MW00439822

In-laws

&

Outlaws

A Door County Cozy Mystery

Book 1

Lilly York

In-laws & Outlaws

A Door County Cozy Mystery

Book 1

©2016 by Lilly York

www.lillyyork.com

Cover Design: Jonna Feavel
40daygraphics.com

Interior Layout: Daniel Mawhinney
40daypublishing.com

Published by: Wide Awake Books
wideawakebooks.com

Also available in eBook publication

The following is a work of fiction. Names, characters, places, and incidents are fictitious or used fictitiously. Any resemblance to real persons, living or dead, to factual events or to businesses is coincidental and unintentional.

Printed in the United States of America

Also by Lilly York

The Willow Crier Cozy Mystery Series

Chili to Die For (Book 1)

I Scream, You Scream (Book 2)

This Little Piggy Wound Up Dead (Book 3)

Southern Fried Son of a Gun (Book 4)

Bobbing for One Bad Apple (Book 5)

The Door County Cozy Mystery Series

In-laws & Outlaws (Book 1)

Catch & Release (Book 2)

Cast of Characters

Hettiger House:

A 100-year-old Victorian house named after the Hettiger family who built it. Rumor has it Miss Mary Hettiger's ghost roams the empty rooms after she was found dead, fully clothed, in bed, holding a red rose. Miss Mary is a direct descendent of Increase and Mary Clafflin, the first settlers of Door County, Wisconsin.

House Proprietors:

Mac MacDonald, husband to Millie, Irish, retired Police Officer with a knack for the details and a horrible Irish brogue. YouTube is his best friend. He insisted all the guest suites must be names after his Family Crest, which holds a place of honor above the large fireplace in the parlor.

Millie MacDonald, wife to Mac, menopausal, professional homemaker who is fulfilling her dream of a bed and breakfast now that the kids are grown and her husband is retired. She tries to keep Mac grounded on the Irish brogue and loves to read— usually mysteries. Agatha Christie is her favorite.

Guests:

The Gold (Honeymoon) Suite: Todd and Susie, newlyweds spending their honeymoon in Door County, Wisconsin.

The Galley Suite: The Perrys, Milwaukee, Wisconsin couple getting away from it all.

The Cross Suite: Mr. Phillips, Chicago businessman looking for investment property.

The Lion Suite: Mr. Normal, nervous gentleman who never told anyone why he was in Door County.

The Fish Suite: Mrs. Hampton, widowed woman visiting family for a reunion.

Uninvited Guests:

Pat and Patty MacDonald (aka—The In-laws)

Locals:

Sheriff Twiggs
Lucy, Hired help
Velia, Lucy's Niece
Chelsea Summers, Librarian
Phyllis, Owns Tower on the Square (famous for their fish boils)
Darla, Real Estate Agent

Chapter 1

Millie MacDonald collapsed, exhausted, onto her and Mac's king size bed. In fact, they both rested their heads against the fluffy down pillows at exactly the same moment.

The amount of work that goes into opening a bed and breakfast is insane, she thought as she tried to get comfortable. Hettiger House had only been open a month but Mac and Millie bought the place over a year ago. Updating the old inn had been a lengthy process. Brother Bay, right next to the iconic Sister Bay in Door County, Wisconsin, was the perfect location for finally realizing her dream. Besides, while the summer months in a northern tourist town were crazy busy, the winter months moved along at a snail's pace. Mac could sit by the fire and write that novel he'd always talked about and they could travel and see the world, another one of their dreams, beginning with Ireland.

She sighed and before she could get comfortable, her husband started snoring. *How does he do that? Does his brain go on strike? Doesn't he think? About anything!* What started as a soft, barely there sleeping wheeze, within seconds transgressed into a loud, obnoxious ground shaking snore. *Great, I'll never get to sleep now.*

Millie gave her husband a light kick then quickly closed her eyes, hoping he would think he woke himself with his snoring. She lay perfectly still, waiting. He was silent for about two seconds before a loud snort erupted from his side of the bed.

"Ugh!" she whispered into her pillow. *Might as well get back up.*

She slipped her feet into her pink fuzzy slippers— her daughter's idea, not hers— and started for their cozy living room. She paused next to her husband and watched his chest rise and fall with each breath. Who was she kidding? She'd give up a kidney to sleep like him. OK, maybe not a kidney. But definitely the spare tire around her midriff. She shook her head and quietly slipped out of their bedroom.

Millie loved the small part of the house she and Mac inhabited. The top floor of the yellow Victorian mansion was all theirs. Their master suite was luxurious. Perhaps not as much as the suites below, but certainly lovely. Besides the master, there was a small guest room, an office, a sitting area, and an eat-in kitchen— certainly enough room for the two of them.

The two floors below consisted of five guest suites, a library, a large kitchen, a parlor, and a dining room. A small office off the kitchen served as command central for the employees she and Mac used to help make the B&B run as efficiently as possible.

The moans and creaks of the old house gave it character. She dismissed the local legend that the place was haunted. Ridiculous. Just because someone died in a residence didn't mean it was haunted. Besides, the old woman had died of natural causes. Or so the story went. Of course, it was also common knowledge that today's crime scene investigators would be able to run tests that weren't available back then. If someone got away with murder there was nothing to be done for it now. Gossips— always speculating.

At the moment, all five guest suites were filled and would be for the next couple of days. Which meant her in-laws' last-minute decision to visit put them in her and Mac's small guest bedroom. They were to arrive the following morning. No wonder she couldn't sleep.

She put the tea kettle on and gathered up some loose-leaf chamomile. *Perhaps that will help me sleep.* Her newfangled electric tea pot turned off and she poured the boiling water over her tea ball, then inhaled deeply of the fragrant steam. She added a touch of honey then blew the hot liquid for a few seconds before taking a sip and settling into her favorite recliner. "Mm…this is good."

She heard the bed groan under the weight of her husband as he turned. She leaned back in her recliner and closed her eyes.

Millie woke with a start and looked around, confused. The sun was already peeking through the blanket of darkness. She jumped and startled the still nearly full cup of tea she'd made the night before.

"Goodness. I'm going to be late with breakfast," she mumbled as she rubbed her sore neck. Mac was nowhere to be seen.

Regardless of running a little late, she took an extra few minutes under the hot shower, hoping that would loosen the stiff muscles in her neck. The smell of coffee penetrated the fresh lemon scent of her body wash.

"Thank you, Mac," she said out loud as she lathered up. A cup would be waiting for her when she descended from the top floor.

She dressed in an early fall, late summer outfit, one that still offered her a reasonable amount of air flow. She hated to wear sleeveless shirts, her arms certainly weren't sculptured, but the least she could reasonably get away with wearing, the better. She slipped a loose-fitting, thin jacket over a tank top. If she got desperate, she could take the jacket off. Menopause wasn't helping. She tussled her curly short mop, thankful for the natural curls she was blessed with, applied some mascara and lip gloss then took off at a quick pace for the lower level.

She entered the large, well equipped bed and breakfast kitchen at full speed.

Mac was at the table with a cup of coffee and the newspaper.

"Woah. Slow down. Take time to smell the roses." He pushed her coffee toward a seat at the table tucked away in the corner of the kitchen.

"Mac, I don't have time to smell the roses. Besides, there aren't any." She turned the oven on then swung back to him. "OK, remind me again why we opened this business. We both hate mornings. Are we gluttons for punishment or what?" She took a big swig of coffee then put her hands on her hips. "Why didn't you wake me up?"

She turned the oven on, then removed the breakfast casseroles and the muffin mix she'd prepared the night before from the refrigerator as she waited for his answer.

"I thought you could use the extra rest. I noticed you went missing after lights out," he said.

"Couldn't sleep, again. Any other time I'd kiss you. But, your parents are due right after breakfast and we have a full house. You should have woke me," she chastised as she checked off items on her mental checklist.

The breakfast sideboard had already been set the night before with Millie's delicate china coffee cups, juice glasses, linen napkins, silverware, plates, and butter.

"Mac, can you get the jams out of the fridge and put them in their serving dishes?" She loved her big commercial stove. She popped both casseroles in one side and the muffins in the other side. She poured coffee, orange juice, and water in their proper containers, making sure the carafe was tightly sealed to keep the coffee piping hot, and carried them to the dining room. She glanced at the time—45 minutes until breakfast.

Mac filled some antique dishes with homemade blackberry, cherry almond, and cherry apple jams. He also placed a dish of apple butter on the buffet. "Where's Lucy?"

Millie shook her head. "I don't know. She didn't call to say she'd be late. I'll chat with her after breakfast—if she shows up that is."

Lucy was their kitchen help. She was at least 10 years older than Millie, if not more, but no one dared ask. She was a feisty little spitfire who had more energy than some teenagers Millie had come across. Sometimes she was downright rude. Just her nature. The woman had a heart of gold if a person looked close enough. She just knew how to hide the fact and was awfully good at doing so.

Usually, Lucy was reliable. And she was a local in need of a job. Social security wasn't cutting it. Millie's forehead creased with worry. In the past month she'd come to rely on the old biddy. Not only for kitchen help but the woman knew everything about everyone in their small bay town. She gave Millie the scoop on the inn. Every last sordid detail. Even speculated that the old woman who had died some hundred years before did not die of natural causes, but was murdered. She said the proof was in this house—somewhere. That's why the place was supposedly haunted. Not that Millie believed a word of it.

The back door creaked open. Lucy made her grand entrance. "Sorry I'm late. My cat went missing. Darn thing. Makes a run for the door every time it opens. I think she thinks she's being held against her will." She thought about it a couple of seconds then added, "I guess she's right." She piled her long, grey hair on top her head and secured it with a couple of big pins. "I would have called but I thought the time would be better spent finding the cat. What else needs doing?"

Millie opened the oven to check the muffins. "You can start slicing the fruit."

Lucy washed her hands then jumped in and got right to work. "You remember what tomorrow is?"

Mac responded, "I sure do."

Millie looked at her husband and mumbled, "Since when do you follow the local gossip?"

He was obviously proud to know something she didn't. "According to Lucy, it's not gossip. It's local legend: 100 years ago, right after this house was built, Miss Mary Hettiger, a direct descendent of Increase and Mary Clafflin, the first settlers of Door County, was found dead on her bed. She was dressed real pretty with a rose in her hand. Now, her death was ruled natural causes but everyone knew something fishy was going on. Who put the rose in her hand? Why was she lying on the bed like snow white?" He leaned into his wife and wiggled his eyebrows as he continued to repeat everything he'd been told. "She's the one who haunts the place."

Millie rolled her eyes. "Quit talking nonsense. You're just doing this to get her going and you know it."

Lucy piped up. "He knows truth when he hears it. You'll see. Somethin' bad's gonna happen. Mark my words." She stuck her bony hip out and patted it. "My bones know these things. Some people's old bones predict the weather, mine predict bad happenins."

Millie ignored both of them and finished getting breakfast on the buffet in the dining room. Everything was in its place when the first guests arrived. "Good morning. I hope you slept well."

The radiant bride vigorously nodded her head and smiled.

The newlyweds, Todd and Susie, inhabited the bridal suite. She was surprised they didn't order breakfast to be served in their room. Most young couples did. These two looked like they were barely out of high school. Although they had been in residence for nearly a week. Perhaps they were ready to interact with other humans. "I'm so glad you two could join us this morning. Everything is ready. Just help yourselves. We do breakfast buffet-style here in the dining room." She noticed the bride managed to blush.

Millie watched Mac go into Irish mode. His voice deepened by a couple of decibels and that Irish lilt magically attached itself to each word spoken. Of course, it was even worse when he led guests into the sitting room and explained the MacDonald crest in the place of pride above the fireplace mantle. That would come later. She was sure of it. Todd seemed to be hanging on his every word.

The others should be here soon, Millie said to herself. She realized some of the bed and breakfasts delivered the morning meal each day to their guests. Millie wanted that old-fashioned gathering to get to know those staying under her roof. Of course, if the guests insisted they wanted a private breakfast, then she acquiesced. But she encouraged them to join the breakfast gathering with the enticement of traditional Irish folk lore. Told in Irish brogue, naturally.

Todd and Susie, the newlyweds, were seated and already eating when Mrs. Hampton, a single woman visiting family in the area, gingerly picked up her plate and began to fill it.

"How are you this morning, Mrs. Hampton?" Millie couldn't help but admire the woman's healthy physique. She was a very pretty woman. Her short grey hair curled slightly, framing her nearly wrinkle free face. Her hands clearly were the only part of her that gave away her age. Dotted with age spots the translucent texture and bulging veins were a dead giveaway. Millie glanced at her own hands, realizing hers weren't too far behind Mrs. Hamptons. Millie guessed she was in her mid-sixties.

"Just fine dear. Just fine. Breakfast looks lovely. I'm so glad I chose to stay here. Heaven knows what I'd be getting if I'd stayed with my relatives." She added a square of the sumptuous casserole to her daintily filled plate then topped her muffin with cherry apple jam before sitting across from the newlyweds. Her voice carried across the room. "Am I in the haunted room?"

Millie carried her juice and coffee for her and set them beside her plate. "Mrs. Hampton, our inn isn't haunted."

"But, is my room the room where that dear woman died with a rose in her hand?" She sighed. "It's so romantic. She probably died of a broken heart. Maybe the rose was his parting gift to her." Mrs. Hampton closed her eyes and breathed in deeply. "This very well may be my favorite moment of the day." She took a sip of the hot coffee and seemed to savor it.

Susie whispered, "I didn't know the inn is haunted."

Millie just shook her head. There was no point in correcting her. People believed what they wanted to believe no matter what they were told.

Lucy appeared with a tray, rolling her eyes. "The Perrys asked for breakfast to be delivered to their suite." She loaded up two plates with the various offerings and set off for the second-floor mumbling and complaining as she went.

Millie wondered about the nice couple from Milwaukee. They were either out and about or sequestered in their room. She hoped she would get to spend some time with them soon.

Right after Lucy left with her delivery, Mr. Phillips, the business man from Chicago, stormed into the dining room. "Have to hurry. You have anything I can just take with me? A to-go cup with coffee, maybe?"

"Oh, yes, I'll be right back." Millie filled a disposable coffee cup with the local brew and a disposable covered dish with a couple of muffins and some fruit. "Perhaps you can eat when you get where you're going." She tucked some plastic silverware in the container as well as a napkin and handed them to the pacing man.

"Oh, thank you. Perhaps tomorrow I'll be able to sit down and enjoy your wonderful breakfast. Sunday's my day off. I won't have anything to do but relax."

Mac spoke up in his best Irish accent. "And a good breakfast ye shall have."

Mr. Phillips startled slightly then realized it was part of the Irish charm the inn described on the website and relaxed. His attempt at an Irish reply came out between an English and an Australian accent, "Then I shan't wait for the morrow then." He laughed as he turned to leave.

Millie watched Mr. Phillips exit the dining room and a couple of minutes later she heard his car pull out into the morning traffic. She wondered what his story was. He was devilishly handsome. His blond hair, blue eyes, and impish grin were certain to garner attention. Not even his crooked nose detracted from his good looks. In fact, he might have been too pretty without the nose.

She said to Mac, "That just leaves Mr. Normal." As host and hostess, they didn't sit down to eat until all their guests were eating. Millie could tell Mac was getting impatient. "I'll go check on him."

Just as she reached the second floor landing, she saw Mr. Normal exiting the Fish Suite, Mrs. Hampton's room. He looked up and when he saw her, he blushed.

"Mrs. MacDonald. I was on my way to breakfast when I remembered I'd left my wallet sitting on the nightstand. I accidently opened the wrong suite door. I was just going back to mine now. I'll be right down."

She was surprised Mrs. Hampton had forgot to lock her door. *Oh well,* she said to herself, *People get a little too relaxed in this quaint northern town and forget all the time. Nothing new.* "No problem, Mr. Normal. I'll see you in a few minutes. I called your room but didn't get an answer. I just thought I'd check to see if you were all right. I thought perhaps you'd changed your mind about breakfast."

He stuttered. "And miss one of your breakfasts? I think not." He opened his own suite door and disappeared for a few seconds before joining her on the staircase. His glasses hung low on his nose and he seemed to push them back every few seconds. She wondered why he didn't get them tightened.

Millie made a mental note to make a little breakfast intention card for her guests to fill out. That would take the second guessing out of the equation. So many little things went into making an inn run smoother. She shook her head and murmured, "Thank goodness for trial and error. I sure have a lot to learn."

After Mr. Normal filled his plate, Mac jumped in and loaded his own plate. By the time all this took place, the newlyweds bid everyone goodbye for the day. They were off on a lighthouse tour followed by a trip to Washington Island. Tomorrow they would be leaving their little love nest and getting back to the real world.

Millie finally sat down next to her husband to enjoy her breakfast. At least Mr. Normal and Mrs. Hampton were still seated and enjoying a leisurely meal. "So, what do you two have planned for the day?"

Mrs. Hampton swallowed a bite then answered, "I'm spending the day with my sister and her family. I'm sure I'll come back with a pounding headache. Those grandchildren of hers are hellions. They listen to no one and do nothing but scream all day. The only part of this vacation that is enjoyable is staying at this inn. I can't imagine what my head would feel like if I'd accepted the invitation to stay with them. I shudder at the thought." A horn honked outside the inn. "Oh that must be them." She shook her head. "It used to be rude to sit in your car and honk your horn to get someone's attention. When did people get so lazy they can't come knock on a door anymore?" She stood up. "Thank you for breakfast. It was delicious." She started to walk away then turned. "Oh, and I almost forgot. The rose in my room is lovely. Thank you."

Millie tilted her head as she watched Mrs. Hampton leave. Mr. Normal never answered Millie's question and quickly excused himself, following closely behind the departing woman. Once they were both gone Millie asked Mac, "Do you have any idea what she's talking about?"

"Nope. Not a clue. Someone must love her though if they gave her a rose." He stood up and refilled his plate as the front door jangled open.

Millie sat down and sighed. She could smell the perfume from the dining room. Her mother in law had arrived.

Chapter 2

Millie stood and greeted her in-laws. "Pat, Patty, you made it."

"Well, yes, dear. Of course we made it. Did you expect us not to?" said Patty as she leaned in to air kiss Millie's cheek.

Millie chose not to answer. It was safer that way. Instead, she offered breakfast. "We have plenty. Make yourselves a plate."

Mac kissed his mom's cheek then shook his dad's hand. "Let me get your luggage. You'll be upstairs with Millie and me. The inn is full."

"Oh, fiddle. Two flights of stairs?" Patty smirked and addressed her husband, "I knew we should have brought the RV. It would have fit just fine in the driveway."

Millie went into panic mode. *RV?* Millie pictured the scene from *Christmas Vacation*, only it was her sewer system blowing up, her guests' cars right along with it.

Patty noticed the fright on Millie's face. "Don't worry, dear. We only brought the car. Maybe next time." She waddled to the sideboard and used her fingers to wipe away an imaginary piece of something from the plate before she filled it. "You just can't get good help these days."

Millie rolled her eyes then remembered her own father threatening to smack her eyes out of her head if she ever did that again. She stole a glance at Pat to see if he'd noticed and hoped her own father hadn't been in cahoots with him. He was shoveling breakfast casserole in his mouth so she was pretty sure she was safe.

Lucy began clearing the serving dishes which caused Pat to rise from his chair and hurry in for a fill up. "I could get used to this."

Who knew a simple comment could bring so much grief. Patty gave Millie a dirty look before commenting, "Imagine what you'd look like if you ate this every day."

Millie looked from her round mother-in-law to her belly protruding father-in-law and wondered what on earth she was talking about. She knew darn well this rich food added the pounds on. She was living proof. But neither of them had any room to talk. She stood to help Lucy and refrained from saying a word. She watched Mac's quickly retreating backside. *Smart man.*

Mac reappeared with one suitcase under his arm, and one in each hand. "I'm going to take this to your room. Do you want to go up with me, see where you're going to be?" He stood still for a moment before starting for the stairs. "It's not all that tricky to find our apartment. Just climb until you have nowhere else to go."

Short and sweet. Mac's style. He disappeared leaving Millie with his parents. Millie started for the kitchen. She'd stopped feeling the need to entertain his folks years ago. They would find their way. She asked Lucy, "Do you know anything about someone giving Mrs. Hampton a rose for her room?"

Lucy turned as white as the ghost she proclaimed lived in the three story mansion. If ghosts were actually white, Millie had no idea. "What? What did I say?"

"Someone put a rose in Mrs. Hampton's room?"

Millie shook her head. "Sometimes, Lucy, you scare me. I just said that, didn't I?"

"It's the ghost. I told you something bad was gonna happen."

"Since when is a red rose a bad thing? I'd love to get some of those 'bad' things from Mac." She wiped down the countertop then began mixing the ingredients for snickerdoodles. The wind ushered in fall with a vengeance. Millie peeked out the window, watching the leaves swirling around her backyard. Pretty soon the teens from next door would be knocking to rake. She'd gladly pay them to get out of the chore.

Lucy had already begun making beds and cleaning bathrooms. Mac had a good excuse to skip his chores today, although she doubted he'd use it.

In the dining room she noticed both his parents' plates were still on the table. She stood at the bottom of the stairs and hoped she wouldn't have to call 911. They weren't used to that many stairs. Who was she kidding? She huffed and puffed her way up each time too. She was bound and determined to get in shape. If it took climbing two sets of stairs multiple times a day, then so be it.

Mac came bounding down and grinned. "I think I've got them settled. The climb pushed them over the edge to a nap. We should have the rest of the morning to finish up and perhaps we can claim a nap of our own before dinner."

Her shoulders slumped. "If only. I could climb back in bed now." She rubbed her neck. "It's still sore."

He kissed her cheek. "Let's hurry and get done. I'll rub some ointment on it then you can get some rest. That should help."

She and Mac were taking his parents to the fish boil downtown for supper. It was a standard favorite and only happened on the weekends in the fall. Dessert would be here with her guests.

Early fall evenings required a roaring fire, some warm cookies, hot chocolate, perhaps a glass of wine, and a game of charades. Not all the guests participated, but the more adventurous ones did. Mac loved it, of course. Millie would rather have curled up by the fire with a good book but she was learning to be more outgoing. Mac helped.

An hour later Millie found herself standing in Mrs. Hampton's room. Sure enough, there was a single red rose in a slim vase on the nightstand. Millie stared for a second, then shook her head. Surely, there is a reasonable explanation. There is no ghost. All the sudden she felt hands grab her by the waist and she let out a scream.

Mac busted out laughing. "Gotcha."

Millie swatted him. "You nearly gave me a heart attack."

"I didn't think you believed in ghosts?"

"I don't. You just scared me, is all." She tucked the corners in then covered the luxury sheets with the handmade quilt she'd picked out for this suite. Afterward, she cleaned the bathroom, vacuumed, added a bottle of water to the small hidden refrigerator, and set a piece of fresh chocolate on the pillow for Mrs. Hampton for later. Satisfied, she gave the rose one last look before closing and locking the door behind her.

Promises of a few stolen moments to rest and a dinner of white fish, potatoes, and onions and her mind willingly tucked the rose to a forgotten corner of her mind.

Chapter 3

Millie watched the flames lick the sides of the giant pot then peeled off her sweater. Her in-laws wanted to be up close and personal with the radiating heat. Millie, not so much. These days, heat followed her like a whining child in need of a good nap.

Mac put his arm around her. "Why don't you share some of that heat with me? I'm chilled." He cuddled a little closer. "I'm hungry too." His eyes greedily took in the rising steam and the smoke from the burning wood. "Mom and dad seem to be enjoying themselves. Thanks for being a good sport." He pulled his wife close, despite the flush to her cheeks.

Millie let her eyes wander the crowd. She saw Mrs. Hampton with what looked like a very large extended family. Three young boys were being corralled, or at least their mother looked like she was trying to keep them in line. The tight smile on Mrs. Hampton's face indicated she didn't think the young mother was trying hard enough. Millie caught her eye and smiled. Mrs. Hampton shrugged and looked away.

The crowd was large and some were starting to line up. The large basket of food would be lifted from the pot any moment now and added to paper plates already laden with melted butter, bread, and coleslaw. Just as Millie turned to join her family in the growing line, she glimpsed a man she thought she recognized. "Mac, is that Mr. Normal?" She pointed toward the man in the long trench coat, the hat and the sun glasses. When she looked at him he had taken his sun glasses off. Had he not done so, she probably wouldn't have noticed him. It wasn't odd he was dressed for warmth as it was getting cool outside, at least to anyone not in the midst of a hot flash. "He wasn't wearing that get up when he left the inn. He's one odd duck, ya know?"

Mac wasn't interested in what Mr. Normal was wearing. He was interested in a big plate of fish and a piece of Door County cherry pie afterward. He pulled Millie along.

"We're supposed to have dessert when we get home."

He held up his cherry pie. "Oh this? This is just dessert appetizer. No worries. I'll still have room."

After finding a seat at one of the many tables along the walk, Millie glanced around. She spotted Mrs. Hampton and her family at one of the large picnic tables. And if she hadn't of seen them, she would certainly have heard them. The youngest little guy was trying to climb out of his booster seat and onto the table. He giggled as if the whole thing was a game. Millie found herself drawn to him. He was such a little cutie. The other two were eating their dinner. She watched the young mother hand him off to his father so she could eat. Millie remembered eating many cold meals as a young mother. As she turned her head, she caught a glimpse of Mr. Normal in his trench coat sitting across the street from Mrs. Hampton's family. He stuck out like a sore thumb. What was he doing? And how did Mrs. Hampton not see him?

Millie turned to her own plate and realized she'd missed what Mac had just said. She raised her eyebrows as she put a piece of fish in her butter then popped it in her mouth.

"I asked if you were ready for a piece of cherry pie."

She nodded with a smile. "Of course."

By the time they returned to the bed and breakfast, Lucy had the cookies in a basket and the hot drinks set up for the guests to enjoy. Millie was astounded Mr. Normal walked through the door without his coat, hat, and glasses. She approached him.

"Mr. Normal, why didn't you eat at the fish boil?"

He stammered, "I wasn't hungry. I people watch." He looked around to see if Mrs. Hampton was within ear shot. "So many interesting people in the world, don't you think?" He turned and quickly walked up the stairs, forgoing dessert.

Millie shrugged then joined the other guests for cookies. This was the time of day when they were the most talkative. Mornings usually found everyone in a hurry to get where they were going. Evenings were for relaxing. She poured herself a cup of hot cocoa and sat down in front of the fire. Her in-laws had grabbed a few cookies then went straight for the apartment. She could hardly blame them. They had to be exhausted after the long drive and a full day, even with a nap.

She found herself with Mr. and Mrs. Perry, the couple in the Galley Suite who wanted their breakfast delivered that morning. "Are you enjoying your visit to Door County?"

They both nodded but Mrs. Perry replied, "So far we've seen the inside of our suite. I felt like such a sluggard. I must have slept until after ten."

Her husband squeezed her hand. "Don't you feel guilty. You needed the extra rest."

Millie tried to interpret the look she gave her husband but failed. "We all could use extra rest now and again. That is what vacation is for. Enjoy it." She sipped her hot drink. "Where are you from?"

"Not far. Milwaukee. We just needed a few days away. Door County is simply beautiful this time of year."

His wife interrupted, "When isn't Door County beautiful?"

"True. We just love it here. Come every chance we get."

"Oh? We loved vacationing here and when my husband retired, we decided to start a bed and breakfast. It's something I've always wanted to do."

Mr. Perry asked, "What did your husband do?"

"He was on the police force. A detective in fact."

Both Mr. and Mrs. Perry paused, ever so slightly, then Mr. Perry commented. "Police force, huh? From around here?"

"Oh no, he retired from the Chicago police force just last month. We're so thankful to be out of the big city. I was made for small town living."

This time the couples' faces turned white. Mrs. Perry responded. "I don't seem to be feeling well." She turned to her husband. "Honey, I think perhaps dinner didn't agree with me. If it's OK with you, I'd like to go lie down."

He stood, placing his hand at her elbow. "I'm not feeling the greatest either. Must be dinner." He addressed Millie, "Please excuse us. We don't mean to be bad company but it seems we have a little touch of something." He led his wife up the stairs and out of sight.

Mr. Phillips stood in the doorway and looked around the room. Millie thought he was an interesting looking business man. He'd clearly seen the receiving end of a fist a time or two. His crooked nose testified to that. *I wonder what business he's in.* A wisp of light hair brushed his forehead and hung just a little too long over the ears to be considered a proper businessmen's haircut. She knew that much. *Perhaps he's a self-made man and doesn't care what anyone thinks? Good for him!* She liked him. Good girls always went for bad boys and she got the feeling he was a very good bad boy. She smirked then jumped as she felt warm breath from behind her chair.

"Are you studying our guests, my dear?"

"Mac! You've got to quit sneaking up on me."

"What, and not have the privilege of seeing you jump? Never. That, me lass, is how I know I'm still the one for ya. Tis' only me can get yer dander up... and yer dander down."

"Mac, have you been listening to Irish phrases again on YouTube?"

"Oh, tis' the arrow of disbelief ye being shootin' me with, Lass."

She raised her eyebrows.

He bent down and whispered. "Are you kidding? I'm making this stuff up as I go." He grinned and took off for the fireplace mantle and yet another explanation of the family crest and the names of the suites— in Irish brogue, naturally.

Millie smiled. She'd not seen Mac this happy in a long time. The stress of his job nearly killed him. She sighed in relief. He was happy, healthy, and hers. Not even the striking blue-eyed bad boy in the room could turn her eye. Not when she had Mac.

Chapter 4

Millie ascended the stairs to their apartment ready to put her feet up and relax. Weekends did a number on her, especially when they were full or had needy patrons. This weekend was no exception. Especially with her in-laws visiting. All she wanted was to make a hot cup of tea, fall into her chair, and watch *The Mentalist* which she'd recorded earlier. She opened the door to find her in-laws in the two recliners watching Antique Road Show and her shoulders slumped. Her father in law had a couple of empty beer cans on the television tray next to him. Neither acknowledged her when she walked in the door.

Mac was nowhere to be seen. "Have either of you seen Mac?"

They both grunted what Millie interpreted as no. He was probably in the garden chatting with someone. Mac loved to talk. She put tea water on hoping they would turn the television down, or better yet, decide to go to bed. She glanced at the clock on the kitchen wall; 9:45. Fifteen minutes and the show would be over. She could only hope.

Lucy promised she would be in a little early the next morning and get everything going. She was making her French toast with sausage and bacon. One of Mac's favorites. Millie would actually get to sleep in a little.

She yawned and poured her second cup of tea. Antique Road Show was over and the news was blaring. Neither in-law had moved a muscle. She shut off the kitchen lights and resigned herself to her bedroom. Both of her in-laws had their eyes closed, both were snoring, and there was a strange smell in the general vicinity of her chair. She carefully removed the remote from Pat's hand and turned the volume down. He stirred. She froze. She tiptoed to her room, still trying to hold her breath.

Mille set her cup on the nightstand then felt her face flush. She started waving her hand, trying to create a breeze. *Menopause stinks!* She opened her bedroom windows. The cool lake breeze did a much better job than her hand, so she left them open and settled down with a book. When her tea was gone and she'd read nearly a chapter, weariness won so she changed and snuggled down in the covers. Still no sign of Mac.

She jolted when he said, "Woman, it's freezing in here. I can see my breath."

She looked up and started chuckling. Her husband was fully clothed in a hoodie, a stocking cap and gloves. "Quit being dramatic. It's not that cold in here." She stretched then climbed out to go to the bathroom. "Oooh, you're right, it is a bit chilly. But it's so comfy snuggled down in those covers." She ran for the bathroom then dove back into bed. The comforter was pulled up to Mac's chin. He was also still wearing the hat and gloves. "Seriously, Mac?" She noticed he'd lowered all the windows but one just to prove he really did love her. She kissed his cheek. "Thanks."

"Oh, don't worry about me. I'll just be a popsicle by tomorrow morning."

She cozied up next to him. "So, what were you doing out so late?"

"Just chatting with the neighbors. They can't wait to see what the ghost is going to do tomorrow. Any time the house has been occupied on the anniversary of Miss Mary Hettiger's death, something happens. One time all the entrances were wrapped up tight like a mummy. I guess we'll find out tomorrow if we can't open the doors."

"Oh Mac, that's nonsense. Probably some teenagers playing with people's minds. Ghosts aren't real. Nor do they mummify houses."

He chuckled. "Of course they aren't. But won't it be fun to get all the neighbors wondering?"

She raised up so she could see his face. "Mac MacDonald, what did you do?"

"What do you mean?"

He chuckled and kissed her forehead. "Don't you worry your pretty little head about it."

"Mac, I'm serious. What did you do?"

"Nothing. I didn't do a thing except get you going." He pulled her close and they both settled into the quiet of the night.

Millie's eyes flew open. Assuming a dream startled her awake, she trudged to the bathroom then climbed back into their bed. As she got comfortable, she heard a door slam. She stilled. The guests were all in their rooms and Mac had locked up the house. Who was up at this hour? She glanced at her alarm clock. Just after two. *Probably just someone looking for a snack, Millie. Go back to sleep.* She convinced herself to close her eyes and get some rest. A familiar creak on the stairs to their apartment brought her out of her slumber once more. This time she shot up and turned on the light.

"Mac. Mac. Wake up. Someone's coming up the stairs." She shook her husband who started swinging his arms, nearly giving her a black eye.

"What, what is it?" He jumped out of bed trying to figure out where he was and what was wrong.

"Someone's on the stairs coming up to our apartment. I heard the creak."

He grabbed the baseball bat from behind his headboard and headed to the apartment door. The living room was bathed in darkness. He listened carefully but heard nothing. Millie was right on his shoulder. He turned to her and whispered, "If I have to swing this bat, you're gonna get hit." He shooed her back with his hand.

She took a step back but still close enough she could feel his body heat. He swung the door to the apartment open and nothing. There was nothing.

She motioned he should go downstairs and check.

Mac rolled his eyes but knew he wouldn't get any sleep if he didn't do as she asked. He pointed to the chair then walked down the stairs. A few minutes later he returned.

"Mrs. Hampton was in the kitchen getting some warm milk. She hoped we didn't mind but she was having a hard time sleeping. She said she didn't climb the stairs but, who knows, she might have thought about asking then changed her mind. Can we get some sleep now?"

She nodded then yawned.

He added, "You know, it might have been mom heading to the bathroom. She gets up more than you do."

Millie's eyes were already closing. "Was she going downstairs? You showed her where the guest bathroom is, right?"

"Yes, Dear, I did. Maybe it was our ghost."

"Mac!"

"I'm kidding, go back to sleep."

The alarm clock went off and Millie squeezed her eyes shut, hoping it was a bad dream. No such luck. Her head was throbbing. She needed caffeine in a bad way. The automatic coffee pot had to be one of the greatest inventions of all time. She could smell the strong brew, ready and waiting. She slipped on her robe and padded to the kitchen for a cup.

She simply stared. The pot was empty. As in, gone. She looked for the culprits. Her in-laws.

Mac stumbled out behind her and looked on the scene. He knew she was going to lose it. "Go. Take your shower. I'll make another pot."

She slammed her cup on the table and instantly regretted it when the pulsing in her head rose a degree. Her mother-in-law came out of the bathroom just as she turned to leave the kitchen.

"Oh, someone's grumpy today."

"Perhaps if you'd made another pot of coffee I might not be."

"You expect your guests to make your coffee? How would I know how you like it? Huh, some bed and breakfast this is."

Mac intervened before Millie could respond. "No worries, Mom. I've got another pot on." He added, "What do you and dad have planned for today? Sightseeing?"

Mille trudged toward the bathroom mumbling, "Guests? If you were paying guests you wouldn't be in my apartment drinking my coffee and emitting strange smells in my chairs! Guests my foot. Termites is the better term."

"Millie…" Mac yelled and she shut her mouth. Between her mood swings, her upcoming 50th birthday, no coffee, and early morning risings, she wasn't a pleasant person to encounter first thing. She knew it. Mac knew it. Too bad her in-laws didn't. She shut her bathroom door and turned the shower on full hot.

By breakfast Millie was almost back to her normal self. Her headache was still on the outskirts of her brain, but at least it had subsided. Lucy was true to her word and had the bacon and sausage finished and the French toast on the griddle when Millie showed up.

"You're a Godsend. You know that?"

Lucy's niece had the sideboard already prepped and all that was left to do was wait for their guests. Mac was salivating.

Everyone but Mrs. Hampton was on time. Even the Perrys, who had their breakfast sent to their room the day before, were present and drooling over breakfast. Mr. Phillips had a full plate and was enjoying every bite. Millie smiled. Todd and Susie, her newlyweds, were chatting away in-between bites with Mr. Normal about the sites he should make a point of seeing while in Door County. He was listening politely but his eyes kept drifting back to the dining room entrance, obviously waiting for Mrs. Hampton.

Millie, noticing Mac was pacing, said, "I tried calling her room but she didn't answer. Maybe she's on her way down. I'll give her a couple of minutes then I'll go check on her."

He nodded and refilled his coffee cup.

Millie overheard Mrs. Perry say, "Did you see what the ghost was up to last night? The whole house has been shrouded in fake cobwebs and ghosts are hanging from the trees. The local paper has already been here taking pictures."

Millie gave her husband a stern look. "Mac. Can we talk in the kitchen please?" She waited for him to follow before saying what was on her mind. "You said you didn't do anything!" Not giving him a chance to respond she added, "Who is going to clean up that mess? And why are you so intent on furthering this ghost story nonsense?"

He cupped her face in his hands. "Did you hear what they were saying? The paper was here taking pictures. Do you know what that's going to do for business? I say we jump on it." He quickly changed the subject. "Are you going to check on Mrs. Hampton? She's still not here and I'm hungry." As if she needed further proof, his stomach growled.

"Oh, all right. I'm going." She took the back stairway and stopped in front of the Fish Suite. The door was partially open. She knocked and called out. "Mrs. Hampton, are you coming to breakfast?" She could hear the fish tank burbling and the bathroom door was open with the light off. No response. She didn't want to surprise the older woman and give her a heart attack but seeing the door was already open, Millie gave it a push and walked in the room.

Mrs. Hampton was lying on the bed, in a lovely floral dress, make up on, hair brushed and held back with a barrette, and one single red rose in her hand. Her eyes were closed and she looked peaceful, as if she were Snow White waiting for her prince. Millie approached the bed then reached out to touch her arm, just to give her a little shake.

Her arm was cool to the touch. Millie started to shake. She was pretty certain she was dead. Dead, dead. As in gone. Finished. She looked around the room, nearly in shock half expecting to see a ghost, not that she'd ever admit such a thing. Millie let out a scream that could be heard throughout the whole house. Well, perhaps not the upstairs apartment, her in-laws had scarfed down their breakfast then returned to the comfortable recliners with the television volume at an all-time high.

Mac was the first to reach her. When he saw what she was screaming about he checked Mrs. Hampton for a pulse and getting none, he pulled Millie out of the room and closed the door. His training as a detective kicked in and he instructed everyone who had followed him up the stairs, "No one enter this room. Someone call the police."

Millie heard chatter about ghosts and whatnot and ignored the ludicrous talk. If Mrs. Hampton was dead of anything other than natural causes, it was murder. And not by any ghost but by a living, breathing, human murderer. Mac insisted everyone go back downstairs to the parlor to wait on the police. No one would be leaving the bed and breakfast until after the authorities had questioned them. Mac made sure the door was securely shut then guided Millie down the stairs.

Chapter 5

Mr. Normal, Mr. Phillips, and the Perrys were nervously pacing the floor and whispering among themselves. Only the newlyweds, Todd and Susie, were sitting, calm, and surprisingly quiet. Lucy was ranting about the ghost going too far this time and the in-laws were perched in front of the television upstairs in the apartment clueless. They'd asked for breakfast to be delivered so they didn't have to go down two flights of stairs until their planned outing, which was lunch.

Mac went over the details with Sheriff Twiggs and showed him the Fish Suite then went to collect his parents who had to make the two-flight trip twice in one day. They were not happy.

Millie looked up to see Patty enter the room. She was obviously upset, and with good reason. Millie patted the seat next to her. Finding a dead body was awful. She could hardly believe Mac dealt with murders and murderers the majority of his police days. She didn't know how he did it. Her mother- in-law avoided sitting next to her and took one of the Victorian chairs with the red upholstery.

"Millie, did your breakfast do her in? We were in the middle of watching the Sunday morning news."

Millie's mouth dropped. How could she ask such a thing?

Mac had the good sense to intervene. "Mom, the news will be on again tonight. I'm pretty certain Mrs. Hampton's death had nothing to do with Millie's cooking. You're still living."

Patty's mouth dropped then quickly closed. She didn't say a word. It wasn't often her son spoke to her in that manner. He was raised better than that.

Millie raised her chin ever so slightly in Patty's direction. That shut her up.

Mac squeezed her hand letting her know he was there for her and he'd take care of her.

Sheriff Twiggs called Mac and Millie into the dining room, his temporary office headquarters. He had met them on several occasions over the course of the last year when they were remodeling the bed and breakfast. He liked Mac and was certain that Mac's experience would come in handy.

He smiled at Millie. "How are you doing?"

She blew out a long breath then shook her head. "I don't know. I'm not feeling all that well."

"Yeah, this sort of thing can do that to a person. I'm sorry you had to see that."

"Me too."

He asked them all sorts of questions about Mrs. Hampton, the other guests, anyone new to the house, and Mac's parents. Mac and Millie answered as best as they could.

Millie exclaimed, "Mac, what happened to Lucy's niece? Where did she go? She was helping in the kitchen when I went upstairs and now she's nowhere to be found." She paused. "Lucy called her Mimi. I'm not sure if that is her real name or just a nickname."

Sheriff Twiggs noted the missing girl before moving on.

Millie was surprised when Mac told the Sheriff all about the strange behavior of Mr. Normal, the Perrys, and Mr. Philips. He even threw in something Millie hadn't noticed. Mr. Phillips had been sitting in his BMW in the parking lot across from the fish boil watching Mrs. Hampton. "Mac, I had no idea you were noticing all that. You could have told me."

"And worry your pretty little head? No way. I was hoping I was wrong but I think we have a houseful of characters, perhaps charlatans. At the very least we haven't been told the entire truth."

Sheriff Twiggs piped up, "I'd say. Your Mrs. Hampton isn't even Mrs. Hampton."

Millie was incredulous. "What? But, I always ask for identification when checking in someone."

Mac smiled. "My wife is an innocent. Thirty years on the force and I tried my best to keep my home life separate from work."

The sheriff nodded. "I can understand that. I try and keep the missus safe too. Best that way. Don't want any harm comin' to 'em."

He stuck a toothpick in-between his teeth. Mac figured it was a nervous habit. Most cops had something they did to relieve stress. Some turned to booze and dope. A toothpick was mild. He nodded in agreement. "She probably had a fake id. They're pretty easy to come by."

"But…but…" Millie stammered, "… She's got be at least 65. She's not 18 wanting to go out drinking."

"No, but I think Mrs. Hampton wanted to be discreet."

Mac rubbed his chin. "Mr. Phillips reminds me of some guys from back home. The DiFranco family. Otherwise known as, The Outfit."

Sheriff Twiggs narrowed his eyes. "He's part of the mob? You've got to be kidding me."

"Well, he just reminds me of them. I've dealt with various members of The Outfit over the past 30 years. You get to know the look, know what I mean?"

Millie listened to her husband share his knowledge. He was supposed to be finished with police work. He survived the windy city and all the crime any cop could handle, which was a miracle in itself. A lot of his buddies didn't survive. He kept quiet but she knew. She heard the stories. She wasn't quite as innocent as he thought. Well, perhaps she was in terms of criminal behavior. But certainly not in regards to the danger involved in police work. She had always been quite aware, even if he'd tried to protect her. Of course at that time she feared something would happen to him.

Millie had one question for Sheriff Twiggs. "So, if she wasn't Mrs. Hampton, who was she?"

"I don't know. We know her information on her driver's license wasn't valid. It may take us a little while to figure out exactly who she is. At this point we only know who she isn't." He shrugged.

"Can't you ask her family? She was here for some family reunion or celebration. You know, I don't think she ever said why she was visiting, except to see her family."

He made another note. "Do you know who her family is?"

Millie shook her head. "No. I don't. They were at the fish boil last night though. Someone must know them. The long picnic table was full of them. Must have been at least fifteen people, including the kids." She thought back to the young mom with the three boys. She paid the most attention to her. "One of the young women had short curly hair, fair skin, freckles. She had three young boys, the youngest being around 2. They were a handful. I'm sure anyone who was there would remember them. She was chasing the boys around half the time."

"OK, I'll go down to the tavern on the square and chat with Phyllis. Maybe she knows them." He stood up. "That really helps a lot. Thanks." He was quiet for a few seconds. "Mac, can I talk to you alone for a couple of minutes? Millie, is that all right with you? Are you OK to go back to the parlor by yourself?"

"I'm recovering quite well, Sheriff. I'll be fine." She kissed her husband's cheek before saying, "Mac, I'm OK with it if you are." Then she left and shut the door behind her.

A few minutes later Mac joined her. "How did you know what he was going to ask?"

She smiled. "I'm observant too. I know he knows how much experience you've had with this sort of thing. Only an idiot wouldn't take advantage of that, if he was able that is." She straightened his collar. "And I'm OK with it. You'll only help straighten this out faster so we can get back to normal. Of course, Mrs. Hampton will never know normal again." She sighed. "I feel terrible for her. I wonder what happened."

"Well, as of today, you're looking at the new volunteer deputy. He's getting me a badge and everything. I told him I've still got my piece, so I won't be needing one of those." He grinned. "Sheriff assured me I won't be needing one for the tasks I'll be aiding him in. I'm to leave the gun in the safe." He chuckled. "Fine with me." He whistled as he walked away to lead Mr. Phillips to the dining room.

Chapter 6

Mac sat down next to Sheriff Twiggs with the intention of people reading. The sheriff had a slow, methodical way about him that caused people to open up and share more than intended. Mac's interrogational gift was hearing what people weren't saying—by their actions or the change in timbre of their voice, or any number of habits or inflections they may or may not be aware of. His job in these interviews was to read people. He may not have the answers when they were done, but he would certainly have a feel for who they are as a person.

Sheriff Twiggs began the interview. "Mr. Phillips, what is your purpose for being here this weekend?"

"My company is here looking at buildings. We're thinking of expanding and they sent me to scout the area and look for possibilities."

"What is your relationship with the deceased?"

Mr. Phillips paused briefly, surprise fleetingly crossing his face. "What do you mean, my relationship? I..." He began again, "I didn't know her. I mean, I just met her."

"Why were you parked outside the fish boil yesterday evening? It sure looked like you were keeping an eye on her."

Mr. Phillips smiled, gaining control of his emotions he said, "I wasn't there to watch Mrs. Hampton. I was considering my dinner options then I ended up in a series of phone calls. It was easier to just work from a parking lot rather than try to communicate with fish or pizza in my mouth. Wouldn't be professional, you know?"

Sheriff Twiggs nodded. "Mr. Phillips, that'll be all for now. I'd appreciate it if you stuck around for a while."

After all the guests sat in the hot seat, Sheriff Twiggs and Mac sat contemplating.

The Sheriff asked, "Well, what do you think?"

"All but Mr. Normal are lying." Mac shook his head. "They aren't telling us something. The Perrys are unified in their story, a little too unified if you know what I mean. They don't act like any married couple I know. Mr. Normal is as nervous as an alley cat being chased by a pack of dogs. Mr. Phillips is a smooth operator. He's used to relying on his good looks and charm, and he's gotten away with it most his life. Lucy knows everyone in this town and I don't think she's capable of murder, even if she is as feisty as the day is long. Her niece disappeared but why would she do it? She certainly didn't know Mrs. Hampton. What motive would she have? She's a local. She'd have no reason."

Sheriff Twiggs said, "She's not a local. She moved her a year or so ago. Odd girl if you ask me. But then again, I've got my idiosyncrasies. I'm odd too."

Mac paused then added, "There's something I'm missing. I can't put my finger on it quite yet, but it'll come to me."

Sheriff Twiggs cupped his chin. "I hear you. We'll keep on digging see what we come up with." He stood up. "I'm gonna go back to the office and get these background checks done." He turned back to Mac. "You know what's odd? We're not finding a single fingerprint in that whole room. Not a one. Someone wiped the room down." He stuck his toothpick in his mouth and sauntered from the room.

Mac remained seated for a few minutes reflecting on the man who had just left. He was a tall man, at least 6 foot 5. Thin wasn't quite the right word—downright skinny was more like it. His hair was almost completely white and he wore it long. Little wisps of color were evident of the original shade. His mustache was droopy and his dark, stormy eyes told wordless tales of pain and grief, both personal and professional.

Mac knew those tales. He didn't have to be told. He would take most of them to his grave with him. They were the stories every law enforcement officer knew by heart. He'd worked hard over the years to shield his wife and now, with a heavy heart, evil had surfaced in their home, right under their noses. To say he wasn't happy would be an understatement. He clenched his hands then slowly straightened them, breathing deeply as he did so. "Come on, Mac. Life can go on as before. Just take care of business, man. No time to get maudlin now." He stood, pushed his chair in, and went in search of his wife.

Chapter 7

Millie rinsed her coffee cup. She wasn't sure what was supposed to happen in cases like this but she doubted the sheriff would want anyone to leave town. She had other guests coming on Monday so where her current guests were supposed to go, she had no idea.

Everyone had been questioned and she was waiting for Mac to return to tell her what was happening. Lucy had cleaned up the kitchen, bless her, so Millie waited in their apartment. She would rely on cookies from the local bakery for this evening. She didn't have the fortitude to mix up a batch. She'd probably forget an ingredient in her frame of mind. Better to be safe rather than sorry. She heard the stair step creak and knew he was nearly home. She would pry what was going on from him. He wouldn't be protecting her this time, she's the one who found the body. She had a right to know what was happening.

Pat and Patty had the good sense to go to lunch and do some sightseeing. Millie was thankful. She had a feeling Mac had something to do with that. The bad news was they weren't supposed to leave until this thing had been at least mostly wrapped up or they were without a doubt in the clear. She wondered how they would feel about moving to the Fish Suite. She grimaced. Maybe not. Probably not in good taste.

She knew her husband and body or no body, he'd be hungry. He hadn't been able to eat breakfast. Lucy had wrapped up a good portion of the leftovers and kept them warm in their oven while they were busy with the sheriff. Millie had everything out on the table ready when Mac walked through the door.

He hugged her. "You read my mind. I'm starving."

"I figured you would be. Let's eat then you can tell me what's happened so far."

He studied her for a second or two. "I really don't want you getting hurt and the more you know, the better the chances are of that happening."

"Mac, better I get my information from you than somewhere else. I'm going to find out what is happening."

He nodded. He knew his wife and she was right. She would go digging. She was curious by nature and there was no way she was going to let him and Twiggs handle it on their own. "Fine. After breakfast. I'll tell you everything I've learned so far."

"You mean lunch. As in the meal we are about to partake."

He chuckled. "Yeah, as in the meal we're about to eat. I'll tell you everything after."

"That was delicious." Mac pushed his plate away and refilled his coffee cup. "We found out one good bit of information. Remember that ridiculous get up Mr. Normal was wearing at the fish boil?"

Millie nodded.

Mac continued, "Well, he was hoping Mrs. Hampton, also known as Mrs. Santangelo, would lead him to her husband, the assumed dead second in command to Mr. DiFranco, from The Outfit in Chicago. Perhaps you remember his death was plastered all over the news for a few days, until something bigger came along, that is. It was assumed he went swimming with the fishes. The thing is, they never did find the body. Mr. DiFranco swore up and down he did not have him taken out. He vowed he'd find out who did though and exact revenge. Well, Mr. Normal thinks Mrs. Santangelo isn't being exactly truthful when it comes to her husband's death. He thinks Mr. Santangelo is still alive and kicking. And he doesn't want to pay out life insurance benefits. He's rather nervous about this job because the woman he replaced went missing after tailing Mrs. Santangelo a week. He's only been with her a couple of days.

I don't think he had anything to do with her murder. What would be his motive?"

Millie pondered the information Mac shared then said, "Yeah, I agree. Mr. Normal is way too nervous. Besides, he was a walk in. He didn't have a reservation. He didn't know anything about the ghost stories surrounding this place. How could he know exactly how to place her body? It doesn't make any sense. He's not our guy."

"Well, it's just a work in motion at this point. We still have a lot of investigating to do. Mr. Phillips insists he doesn't know the DiFrancos, and the Perrys insist they are just taking a few day's rest. Both claim they didn't know Mrs. Hampton and had no contact with her before or after coming to the inn. Mr. Phillips didn't have a good explanation for sitting in his car and watching the goings on. He claimed he was deciding if he wanted to join the throng of people or go find someplace a little quieter to eat. He said he was there for a bit because he was on the phone— business calls. He ended up going for pizza. Who knows? I guess we'll find out eventually. We really can't keep them here for that long. Not unless we find something that ties them to Mrs. Santangelo. Otherwise, they're going to fly the coop and they'll be long gone."

"Did the Sheriff find out what happened to Lucy's niece?"

"Yeah. Apparently she has another job and had to leave for work. She called Sheriff Twiggs and gave him her statement. I think she's in the clear. Besides, she's lived here for over a year and had never met Mrs. Santangelo. This being her first day helping out here, I doubt she suddenly up and decided to off someone." He shook his head. "No, I think the mob has something to do with all this. That's what I think."

Millie nodded. "True. I guess I need to rest my head for a little while and think. Do you know when your parents are due back? I'd like to lie down for a little while."

They won't be back until after supper. We can relax.

"Oh, did you remember to tell Sheriff Twiggs about last night? Someone on our steps? Mrs. Hampton, I mean, Mrs. Santangelo having milk before bed?" She scowled. "I'm not sure I'll ever get used to calling her by her real name."

"No, I forgot about it to be honest. I just figured it was her but I think you're right. We better tell him everything. I'll give him a quick call then I'll join you for that nap."

Millie was in bed, nearly asleep, when Mac climbed in. "Mac," she cried. "Why did this have to happen to us?"

Mac pulled her into his arms. "We'll make it to the other side. We always do."

Millie cried herself to sleep lying in Mac's arms.

Chapter 8

Millie needed to think. She needed mindless work that would allow her to ponder the events over the past few days and anything she might have seen or heard that seemed irrelevant at the time. Yard work— that is what she needed.

She slipped out of bed unnoticed by Mac. She stilled when his snoring abruptly stopped then quietly walked to the bathroom when he resumed. She needed work clothes, old jeans, an old T-shirt, and perhaps a flannel button up she could remove when she got too hot. She never knew when a hot flash would attack. She finished her ensemble with an old pair of tennis shoes then headed downstairs for the back yard and the garden shed.

Millie paused when she noticed the door to the shed ajar. She thought she had locked it the last time she'd gone in. Then she shrugged. With everything that had been happening, Mac may have taken out the trash and forgot. Oh well. She opened the door fully so some sunshine would light up the dim space. She located the rake and her garden gloves. After raking she still had some fall flowers that needed pruning, a few more bulbs that needed planting, and soil that needed readying for the winter. Plenty to keep her busy and her mind free. Then she'd be able to pack away her gardening supplies for winter. She started to turn when she noticed one bin of trash had been nearly emptied of its contents. She took a step toward the trash bin when the shed door suddenly closed. She heard the lock click into place and yelled out. "Hello. I'm in here."

No response.

Whoever closed the door either didn't hear her and didn't know she was in the shed, or they knew and wanted to keep her contained. She felt for her phone and realized she left it on the kitchen counter. Nothing to do now but wait. Someone would miss her eventually. And, she had time to think. On the other hand, the leaves weren't getting raked.

Her eyes adjusted as little cracks in the shed allowed some sunlight to seep through. It wasn't much and she'd be in complete darkness after sunset. She heard some scurrying and jumped. "What to do? What to do?" She asked herself.

The first order of business was trying to determine what the garbage collector was looking for. Perhaps they hadn't found it, whatever it was, and she would find it first. She put on her gloves and started separating the trash. First she pulled out the bags from the most obvious place, the bedrooms. It seemed the least likely place the killer— if there actually was a killer— would have the opportunity to throw away incriminating evidence would be in the kitchen trash. Millie stopped her search and nearly smacked herself on the forehead. She was assuming a guest had committed the atrocity. What if that was the wrong assumption? Her shoulders slumped. She'd have to go through every bag.

She began pulling anything that looked even remotely suspicious. By the time she reached the kitchen garbage, she'd found exactly nothing. Not a thing. She emptied the contents and was thankful for the autumn weather. She could imagine the stench this bag would emit in the heat of summer.

Toward the bottom of the bag she found what she was looking for—a syringe wrapped in a paper towel. Now she had to wonder, what was in it and who threw it away in the kitchen trash. *Now, to get out of here.*

Millie figured she'd been in the shed at least a couple of hours. Mac should be missing her by now and looking for her. Which meant he'd be searching the grounds. She started clanking her metal watering can with her spade. The loud tinny noise was enough to give her a headache but at least she'd be found. She hoped. Between yelling and making as much racket as she could, she finally heard rustling and voices. "Mac. I'm in the shed."

"Yes, Dear, we finally figured out where all the noise was coming from." He unlocked the door and hugged her to him. "This, today, not knowing if you were hurt or if someone had done something to you, is what I can't handle. I don't know what I'd have done."

"Oh, Mac. I'm fine. Really. I came down to do some yard work and think, the next thing I know someone is locking me in the shed."

"Did you see who it was?"

"No. I'm sorry. I had my back to the door. I can tell you though what that someone had been doing. They were looking in the trash for this." She held up the syringe.

He took it from her. "Where did you find that?"

"The kitchen trash. Of course, the last bag, and the nastiest bag, I went through."

"Millie, I think you found our murder weapon. Sheriff Twiggs called and said Mrs. Santangelo had a heart attack. He had no idea why anyone would dress her up but he was fairly certain she died from natural causes." He wiped some dirt from her cheek. "I think he might want to rethink that conclusion."

"I think you're right." She walked with her husband back into the house.

"Why don't you go upstairs and hop in the shower and I'll call the sheriff."

By the time Sheriff Twiggs arrived, Millie was comfortable and clean. If he only knew how bad she'd smelled, well, he would be a little more grateful for the evidence she produced and what she went through to get it. A fresh pot of coffee sat ready, as did tea water.

She poured them each a cup of coffee and a cup of tea for herself before she explained what happened. "Perhaps whoever it was didn't hear me. You never know. Some people's hearing isn't all that good."

He looked grim. "No, I don't believe that was it at all. In fact, I think the murderer was going to come back after dark and, well…it wouldn't have been good."

Millie swallowed hard. "As in…finish me off?"

Sheriff Twiggs nodded. "As much as I hate to say it, yeah. It's a good thing your husband went looking for you. Another couple of hours…"

Mac piped up. "We don't know that for sure. One thing we do know, you found the murder weapon and it was most certainly murder, right?"

He looked at the Sheriff. "Yeah, I had our medical examiner go back over the body. It would appear our Mrs. Santangelo was injected under the tongue, where an injection site is just not as obvious. Her symptoms were that of a heart attack, higher levels of potassium chloride, but that is to be expected." He held up the syringe. "My guess is this will prove she had help having that heart attack." He added, "You made it clear that I was picking this up, right? I wouldn't want there to be another attempt to recover what was thoughtlessly discarded."

Mac responded, "Yeah, I made sure word got around you were coming."

"Good. That should help keep you safe, Millie."

She raised her eyebrows. "Help?"

The sheriff had the good sense to shrug. There were no guarantees in life.

She nodded in agreement. "I suppose, you're right. What else can we do?"

"Well, short of catching the person who did this, stay on guard. Be aware of your surroundings and let your husband know if you plan on taking off on your own."

Mac stood behind his wife and placed his hands on her shoulders. "We'll take every precaution."

The Sheriff asked to speak to Mac so Millie took her tea and moved to the patio off their bedroom, her favorite place in the whole house. She loved having guests. She loved a full house. But, she also loved her quiet time. The bay was directly across the street. In the quiet of the nighttime she could hear the water brushing up against the sandy beach. As sunset neared, the town interfered and usually masked the sounds coming from the water brushing up against the shore.

Sailboats dotted the calm bay as the sun hung low in the western sky. Between the sunset and the glorious fall colors, Millie nearly forgot about her close call in the shed. She sipped her tea, thankful that her day didn't get any worse.

As evening approached, temperatures dropped and she pulled her sweater a little tighter. Mac appeared a few minutes later and sat down next to her on the free-standing swing.

"Are you OK?"

She nodded. "I was never really that worried until everything was said and done. That's when I thought about what could have happened and what whoever locked me in the shed might have planned for later." She squeezed his hand. "How could the killer not know you'd be looking for me?"

"Yeah, I've thought about that too. I think it rules out anyone who knows us."

"So, what, we've ruled out your parents and Lucy." She added, "Which we pretty much already knew. I guess we're no farther than we were before I was locked up in the shed."

"That's not true. You had the good sense to figure out the killer was looking for something and found the syringe. An animal could have toppled that garbage. Perhaps that's what he wanted you to think."

"True. We now know Mrs. Hampton, or whatever her name is, was killed with potassium chloride by a human and not a ghost."

Mac chuckled. "Try telling that to Lucy. She's insisting it's a ghost out for revenge. Apparently, we cannot book that room on the anniversary of the original murder—and yes, she's insisting the first death was a murder—and the victim's ghost will exact revenge. There is no arguing with her."

"Lucy's crazy."

"She is interesting, that's for sure. What did you think of her niece? I didn't even catch her name."

"She was sure quiet. I barely got a murmur out of her. I guess they call her Velia. I've never heard it before. I'll have to ask Lucy about her. She certainly doesn't take after her aunt. That woman never stops talking."

His stomach growled. "I ordered pizza for dinner." He glanced at his watch. "Should be here any minute. I figured you weren't in the mood to cook or go out. How about we watch some television and prop our feet up."

She'd already decided it would be take out for supper. She simply didn't have the energy to cook. Her in-laws could eat with them or go out, she wasn't going to worry about it. And she was reclaiming her recliner. Well, after fumigating it. She was surprised they hadn't returned for the day. *Oh well, they're grown-ups, they can take care of themselves.* "Pizza sounds perfect."

Chapter 9

The clock chimed 9 pm. Millie's feet were propped up in her now pumpkin scented recliner and she lightly snored as Mac tried to locate his parents. He'd called several times with no luck. Finally he called the Sheriff who promised to keep one eye out for them. Just in case. Best to be safe than sorry.

He settled down in his own chair and flipped through some channels. He settled on the history channel.

The knock at the door an hour later startled both her and Mac awake. He jumped up and answered the door, hoping it was his parents.

Sheriff Twiggs stood on the other side flanked by none other than Mac's parents. "I take it these two belong to you?"

Mac, normally not a person short on words, stuttered. "Yes…where did you find them?"

"Well, we asked everyone to stick close until we could clear them. We caught these two sneaking out of town, bags packed and driving south."

Mac's mouth dropped. "Mom? Dad? What were you doing?"

"Well, your father has a doctor's appointment tomorrow. If we aren't back then he'll have to reschedule. The last time it took almost six weeks to get an appointment. It's just silly keeping us here." She crossed her arms, as if that was explanation enough.

"Mom, there was a murder. This is a murder investigation. When you go sneaking out of town, it makes you look guilty."

Pat harrumphed and Patty looked offended. "We didn't kill anybody. Why, I never. The very idea…"

Mac shook his head and pointed to the door to the guest room. Both walked in with their bags murmuring like petulant teenagers. He addressed Sheriff Twiggs. "I'm really sorry about that. I'm certain they didn't have anything to do with the murder but, I completely understand. They need to follow the rules like everyone else."

The sheriff grinned. "I figured you two didn't know anything about it." He shook his head and grinned. "Keep 'em locked up if you got to. I'll try and let 'em out of here early tomorrow morning so they don't miss their appointment. I'd hate for your dad's hemorrhoids to get any worse."

Mac felt his face flush. "Already gave you a rundown of the appointment, did they?"

"You betcha. Heard all about it. Didn't even have to ask." He took his hat off when he noticed Millie still in the recliner. "How you doing, Millie? Better?"

She lowered her feet and stood. "I'll live. At least I don't have to worry about the couple of rooms that were reserved. Seems both rooms were for the same party and they cancelled. So we've dodged a bullet there."

"Well, that helps. Although it doesn't help your pocketbook. I know every dime counts, especially these days."

"We'll be fine. No worries. Just find out who killed that poor woman. I want to feel safe in my own house again, ya know?"

He nodded. "Will do, Ma'am." Sheriff Twiggs turned to Mac. "I'll see you tomorrow morning then."

***

Mac walked the Sheriff downstairs so he could lock up after him.

Mac asked, "Did you get the background checks back on all the guests?"

"Not all. Some. Mr. Normal does indeed work for the insurance company and yes, he was investigating her claim. Mr. Phillips is a businessman from Chicago although he has affiliations with The Outfit. We're not sure if it's really a business trip that brought him this far north or if his trip had more to do with Mrs. Santangelo. He's looking into a resort that's up for sale, so perhaps his trip is legit. Then again..." Sheriff Twiggs shrugged and shifted his toothpick. "The Perrys don't seem to be who they say they are. I'm workin' on it and should know soon. They are proving to be a little harder to pin down." He turned to go then called over his shoulder, "I'll give you a call as soon as I know more."

Mac waved goodbye and locked the door. If any of the guests were still out they'd have to use the key code to re-enter. He wasn't leaving the doors unlocked this evening, not with a killer on the loose.

He decided to check the downstairs to make sure everything was as it should be. When he was on the beat in Chicago he had diverted many disasters simply by remaining aware. It wouldn't pay to relax his standards now. A 30 year habit was hard to break, and his primal instinct of protecting hearth and home was on high alert. He loved retirement and while he could do without his wife being in danger, he had to admit he missed the chase. It was in his blood. Not this close to home of course, but, perhaps he could lend a hand to Sheriff Twiggs if ever the need arose.

He moved from room to room checking doors and windows. Everything seemed to be in order. At least in the house. As he checked the backdoor he saw a stream of light near the shed. Who would be running around their backyard with a flashlight? He was glad he hadn't turned on the kitchen lights. Whoever it was had no idea they had been spotted. He opened the backdoor wishing he'd oiled the hinges. When Millie had asked him, he hadn't thought it was high on his list of priorities. He mentally moved it up on his 'honey do' list.

The light suddenly disappeared and a figure cloaked in black popped out of the shed. Mac knew he'd locked it up. Who was getting into their shed? He was certain alerting the public to the syringe being found would put a stop to the criminal intruder. He'd been wrong before and he was certain he'd be wrong again.

The figure took off running and Mac called out after him. Or her. Between the darkness of night and the dark clothing, he really couldn't tell. "Hey, stop." He was no longer in any shape to go chasing after anyone. He turned on the garden lights and grabbed his own flashlight, eager to see what he'd caught the criminal in the middle of.

The shed was in disarray. "What in the world were they after?" He said out loud to himself. He was surprised to hear a voice behind him so he jumped and hit his head then turned. "What are you doing here?"

"I was going to ask you the same thing?" The young officer looked accusingly at Mac.

Mac stuttered, not used to being questioned why he was rummaging around his own shed. "I live here. Didn't you see the guy who was here before me?"

"No, Sir. I only saw you when the motion lights went on." He paused. "Then I saw you with a flashlight. I already called it in. Sheriff should be here any minute."

Mac turned when he heard Millie.

"Mac, what's going on? I saw the back yard lights turn on." She approached her husband. "What is he doing here?" She asked of the uniformed officer.

"Ma'am, I was here watching over the house. Quiet like so as not to give myself away. Sheriff wanted to make sure you were safe." He gave Mac a condemning look before showing concern once again to Millie. He heard a noise behind him. "Sheriff's here now. He'll take care of this interloper."

Millie's mouth dropped but before she could say a word Sheriff Twiggs spoke up. "Mac, Millie, what's goin' on?"

Mac and the young officer started speaking at the same time. Sheriff Twiggs raised his eyebrows and the officer clamped his lips shut. Mac continued. "I saw someone out here with a flashlight. I tried to open the door…"

Millie interrupted. "That darn creak. Mac, I asked you to oil that door."

He purse his lips. "Yeah, I know. In any case, the door made enough noise to alert the intruder so I turned on the back garden lights to see if I could identify him. He was dressed in all black and ran when the lights came on. I thought I'd try and see what he was up to. Someone sure likes the inside of my shed. I have no idea what they were doing. Nothing seems amiss."

The officer took the pause to mean he could speak. "Sir, may I?"

Sheriff Twiggs twirled his toothpick and nodded.

"I saw a flashlight beam and was about to investigate when I saw him…" he nodded toward Mac, "…flashlight and all when the motion detector lights went off. I say he's our perp."

Mac nearly shouted. "You told me you didn't see anyone before you saw me. Now you say you saw someone with a flashlight. And for the record, these lights aren't motion activated. They turn on with a light switch." To prove his point he marched back to the house and turned the lights off. He yelled back to the group. "Move around. You'll see. They won't turn back on until I flip the switch."

The young police officer waved his hands then looked around sheepishly.

Mac turned the lights back on and stomped back to the group. "So, how could I be in two places at once? Huh? I turned the lights on. Who had the flashlight?" He glanced at the long blue mag light in his hands. "Not mine, the other one?"

Sheriff Twiggs waited until everyone quieted down. "Looks to me like all this ruckus scared the guilty party off. Probably won't be showing his face around here again tonight. Why don't we all get some rest then come back here tomorrow in the daylight and figure out what is so interesting about this here shed. Seems to me nothing is as it appears." He addressed his charge. "You continue to watch. This time, make sure you investigate before the owner of the house has to do all your work for ya."

"Yes, Sir." The young officer returned to the unmarked car parked on the side street adjacent to the back yard where he could watch and wait.

"Sorry about that. He's young and trying to impress. You must remember those days."

Mac harrumphed and grudgingly agreed. He did remember, all too well. He didn't have to like it though. "I don't like being accused of murder or intending to do my wife harm. But yeah, I remember. Not my best days, for sure."

"I'll be back first light. Let's figure out why this old dilapidated shed is of such interest." He tipped his imaginary hat and sauntered away, leaving Mac with his blue flashlight and Millie in her house coat and slippers staring at one another.

"Mac, what just happened?"

He put his arm around her and led her back to the house as he told her the whole story.

Chapter 10

Mac and Millie were up before the sun—not exactly their choice. His parents had retired early and both were up making such a ruckus that neither of them could sleep, not that sleep had been easy coming. Millie had thought about the shed long after the lights went out.

After numerous cups of coffee and a simple breakfast of toast and jam they both descended the two flights of stairs to meet Sheriff Twiggs. It was past time to find out what was so interesting about a shed.

Mac and Millie were rummaging around the building when the Sheriff appeared. "You two find anything yet?"

"Nope. Not a thing." Mac tossed an old bucket to the other side of the building. It wasn't large, per se, but it was odd shaped. "I did find a whole stack of old newspapers. Thought I'd keep 'em and read through 'em. Great way of learning the history of a place."

Millie nearly growled. "Mac MacDonald. We don't need more stuff sitting around the house."

"I'll hurry through 'em and throw 'em out as soon as I'm finished. And I'll keep 'em in my truck, deal?"

"Fine. You want to read in your truck, you go ahead."

"Deal." He tucked the newspapers in the cab and got back to the Sheriff.

The sheriff suggested, "Why don't we get everything out of here? Maybe then we'll see something that pops out at us."

They made an assembly line and removed all of their lawn tools, gardening paraphernalia, the odd bins of whatnots and the rusty junk Mac had meant to go through and just hadn't got to yet. He began to fill the wheelbarrow to load up his truck for the dump. After numerous trips everything worth keeping was decorating the lawn and everything else was piled high in the bed of his pickup.

All that was left was a bunch of built in shelves splintering from years of neglect and an odd shaped box, most likely to store wood in for heating the house.

All three turned in a circle. They saw nothing that raised any eyebrows when they removed the contents and now, down to bare bones, there was nothing of interest either.

"Well, at least the shed will be organized now." Millie started to turn but tripped on a board that was slightly higher than the other boards around it. She landed in Mac's arms.

"I guess that's another project for me. Funny how we never noticed it before."

"I think one of those bins was resting there. We wouldn't have noticed. Not with a full shed."

Mac bent down to see if he could push the board downward so no one got hurt when he noticed the board wasn't part of the floor. It was almost handle-like in nature. It was attached to a bottom board. "What the dickens is this?" He lifted it up and a square section of wood lifted, all one piece, all at once. "This is a door. And there are steps under this. How did we not see this when we moved all our stuff in here?" He glanced at Sheriff Twiggs. "Looks like we found a hidden tunnel. I wonder where it leads."

"You have your flashlight handy?"

Mac ran to the kitchen then returned with his trusty mag light. He looked at Millie, expectantly, and she shook her head. She'd seen too many scary movies. She wasn't about to climb down a set of steps that led to who knows where. The killer could be watching and perhaps they'd be trapped and forced to die a slow, horrible death. "You go. I'll stay here and keep watch."

Both Mac and the Sheriff disappeared down the dark hole. Millie heard them on the descent but it didn't take long for silence to fill the air. She patiently waited for them to reappear and they did, just not as she expected.

Mac yelled out. "Millie, over here."

She quickly turned around to see both her husband and the sheriff standing outside the kitchen door. She tilted her head in confusion but travelled the distance to the door. "How did you get here?"

He grinned. "Come on, we'll show you."

She followed the grinning boys to the barely used library where a book shelf was turned perpendicular to its shelf mates. "A secret passage? Really? But why?"

Mac shrugged, still grinning like a kid at Christmas. "Isn't it awesome?"

"Mac! Awesome? This is how someone has been getting in our house. Or perhaps out of our house. We don't know. We're no closer to the truth, in fact, if we really think about it our suspect pool just got a whole lot larger. How many people in town know about this? And how do we find out who does?"

"Hmmm…" Sheriff Twiggs rested his index finger around his toothpick. "I have an idea on where to start. Our librarian, Chelsea Summers, considers herself to be a local history buff. If anyone knows anything it would be her. Or at least where to find some answers." He raised his eyebrows. "Want to go with me?"

Mac yelped, at least Millie thought he yelped as he took off out the front door with the sheriff, leaving her to wonder what in the world to do with an open book shelf and all their shed inhabitants littering the lawn.

She heard Lucy puttering around the kitchen, getting breakfast ready for their guests. Not so much guests as murder suspects. Millie sure hoped the new housing the sheriff lined up would be ready soon. Having them still in her house was costing her a bundle. Not only did she not have any rooms available for drop-ins, but she was also still feeding the group. A little hotel on the outskirts of town was getting some rooms ready. Thankfully they would be on their own soon. Unless of course they wanted to remain and pay her to keep their current comfort status. Some extra income wouldn't be unwelcome. Of course the idea that one of them could be a murderer gave her pause. Then again, it could be anyone in town. The secret passageway was evidence of that. The sheriff would have to let everyone go soon. He couldn't hold them without some kind of evidence.

She joined Lucy in the kitchen.

"What happened to the shed?"

Millie sighed. "Another break in. This time we thought we'd figure out why they were so interested in our shed. We found the answer."

Lucy stopped what she was doing. "Well? You gonna share?"

"There's a secret passageway from the library to the shed. Who knew? Seems someone sure did. And they've been using it to pass back and forth to the house."

Lucy's mouth was slightly ajar. "You've got to be kidding me. Huh. Wonder why they put that in?"

Velia chose that moment to walk out of the pantry.

Millie smiled at her. "I didn't realize you were here. I don't think we've been properly introduced."

The girl nodded but didn't say anything, she looked to Lucy.

"Speak up, Child. Cat got your tongue?"

Velia did as her aunt asked. "I'm Velia."

Millie had no idea the girl was so shy, so she kept it short. She wasn't shy, herself, but one of her children would turn inward the second a stranger laid eyes on her. Now that she was an adult it wasn't quite so bad, but when she was younger she avoided any type of face to face no matter what the cause. She knew being put on the spot was hard for some. "Well, it's good to have your help. We sure are thankful. With everything going on we can use an extra pair of hands."

The young woman remained stoic. Millie, not exactly sure what she could say to make the girl feel comfortable, left the two of them alone and went off to close up the library. She still wanted to ask Lucy about Velia though, as soon as they had a free moment together.

Her in-laws were descending the last of the stairs as Millie rounded the corner for the library.

"Do I smell breakfast?"

Millie replied. "You sure do. Lucy's almost finished. It'll be ready soon."

Patty helped herself to a cup of coffee and sat down next to her husband at the long dining room table. Both had already had a small breakfast in the early morning hours. Millie had to concur and allowed herself to be distracted. Her stomach was rumbling too. Cleaning out a shed and finding a secret passage way made a person hungry. She sniffed the air appreciatively.

This morning, all the guests but the Perrys arrived downstairs at the same time, muttering amongst themselves as they meandered into the dining room. Millie looked around for the couple who had been inhabiting the Galley Suite. They had been kind of funny about eating with everyone else. Perhaps they wanted room service again. She joined Lucy and Velia in the kitchen. "Lucy, did the Perrys ask for a tray?"

"Nope. Not a word from either of them. Maybe they're on their way down."

Millie scrunched her face, thinking about the elusive couple. She wondered why they were so secretive.

Velia added yogurt parfaits and granola to the sideboard while Lucy carried in platters of scrambled eggs, sausage, and breakfast ham. The toaster was in full swing as bagels and English muffins passed through and onto various plates.

Her father in-law, never one to be shy, was first in line. He and Patty were the only ones chattering about like nothing had happened. Everyone else continued to watch each other throughout the meal.

Millie figured it best to address the elephant in the room. "Sheriff Twiggs has reserved rooms for each of you at the Ace Motel on the outskirts of town. The rooms are all the sheriff's office can afford. Of course you are welcome to stay here but you will have to pay the normal room rate. I'm expecting to hear from the hotel sometime this morning so if you want to move over there, just start packing your things. You can hang out down here in the parlor until the rooms are ready. We need to get the rooms clean so we can rent them out."

Mr. Phillips was the first to speak up. "If you don't mind, I'd rather stay here. I'm thinking the Ace Motel sounds rather... basic, to speak kindly."

Millie nodded. That was being kind. She looked to the other guests.

Susie, the blushing bride asked, "Do you know how long the Sheriff plans on keeping us here?"

"No, I'm sorry I don't. I know he's working as hard as he can to get to the bottom of all this. He'll be here in a little while. Why don't you ask him then?"

Susie looked away, not happy with Millie's answer.

Todd added, "We'll be staying here as well."

Mr. Normal was the only one who hadn't revealed his intentions. "I guess I'll stay too. At least we'll be able to keep an eye on each other. It's obvious the sheriff thinks one of us is the murderer."

They all glanced at one another wondering who did the evil deed.

Millie came to the Sheriff's defense. "He has to question all of us. Not just you. My in-laws aren't allowed to leave yet either. She glanced their way to see if they appeared in the least way embarrassed at having tried to sneak off. Nope. They were busy eating, not paying attention to a word she said.

She walked back into the kitchen. "They're all staying here. I better let the sheriff know." She started for the phone then stopped. "Lucy, can you make a grocery store run? We're gonna need some staples for the next couple of days."

Lucy nodded as she washed dishes.

"Where did Velia go?"

Lucy looked up. "I sent her out to the green house for some herbs. She'll be back in a minute or two."

Millie looked around to make sure she wasn't overheard. "Your niece is really shy."

"Well, she's not really my niece. I just call her that."

"Oh, I didn't know that. Why?"

"I guess she just attached herself to me and I ended up thinking of her like a niece. She doesn't have any family and well, she looks to me as if I'm her family." Lucy shrugged and continued washing the fry pans stacked up next to the large sink. "She's more devoted than my real nieces and nephews, that's for sure. She'd do just about anything for me. It's good to have someone in your life you can depend on."

Millie nodded in agreement then took her leave.

After breakfast Millie was about to help start cleaning the guest rooms when a knock at the door changed her plans. She opened the door to Sheriff Twiggs as Velia came bounding down the stairs saying, "The Perrys are gone."

Sheriff Twiggs looked toward the young woman in expectation. "Tell us what you know, young lady."

She nodded. "Their room has been packed up. Everything is gone, well, almost everything. Looks like they ran out in a hurry too. They left this behind." She held up a small notebook. "I found it under the arm chair next to the bed."

Sheriff Twiggs took the notebook from her and turned the pages, whistling under his breath as he did so. "The Perrys did indeed make a run for it. They thought dealing with a small town sheriff was going to be a walk through the park. Guess they had another thing coming. They're already in lock up." He asked Millie. "Mac back yet? He's gonna want to hear this too."

"I haven't seen him since he took off with you. Where'd he go?"

Mac's parents, Pat and Patty, appeared with their bags in hand. "Sheriff, you said we might be able to head home this morning so I can make my appointment. You decide if that's OK?"

Sheriff Twiggs looked down and kicked a rock then sighed. He opened his mouth to speak as Pat's phone started ringing so he clamped it shut and listened to the one sided conversation.

"Yes, you're speaking to 'em. Yes. Uh huh, OK. Well, I'll see you next week then." Pat tucked his phone in his front pocket, picked up his bags, and said, "Come on, Patty. Looks like we get a few more days with the kids." He dropped his bags in the hallway by the staircase and headed for the kitchen.

Millie looked at Sheriff Twiggs and just lifted her shoulders as if to say, who knows.

Mac's truck pulled up in front of the house and both Millie and the Sheriff waited for him.

Twirling his toothpick the sheriff said, "Mac, looks like the Perrys tried to make a run for it in your boat."

"My boat? How in the world did you catch them?"

"Oh, I had a funny feeling someone was going to try to make a quick getaway. I had that young kid who cornered you in the shed watching the house while I had another keeping a lookout on your boat. I figured the boat was too big a temptation. Easy getaway. Looks like I figured right." He grinned. "I was about to tell your folks they could head on home when he got that phone call. You can let 'em know the good news." He glanced at his watch. "They can head on home if they want to. Well, I've got work to do down at the station so I best be moving on. Thanks for your help." He tipped his imaginary hat them sauntered down the sidewalk to the parked cruiser.

Mac shut the door behind Millie. "Huh. What do you think of that?'

She shook her head. "Does this mean everyone else is free to go to?"

Mac shrugged. "I guess so. Sheriff seems to think he got his man. Err…man and woman in this case."

Millie started for the kitchen. "I've got to catch Lucy before she leaves to go shopping."

Chapter 11

Mac watched Millie's retreating backside disappear, then he headed for the library and the secret passage. He didn't buy the Perrys being the guilty party. There's no way they knew about this passage. At least he was pretty certain they couldn't have. When the Sheriff got called away, Mac went on to chat with the librarian. He'd learned a few things about local history but she had no idea a secret passageway had been included in the old inn nor did she know anyone who might know. She'd once heard a rumor that the old house plans had been found but nothing ever came of it and she'd never seen them. She didn't know where the rumor started. Small towns worked that way. Someone heard something from someone who'd heard it from someone else. No one knew who started the whole rumor. During remodeling the carpenter didn't notice it. So it couldn't have been an easy find. Whoever had access to the tunnel had to have had an opportunity to find it—or plans showing them exactly where the secret passageway began and ended.

He slipped through the secret opening then quietly closed the book shelf behind him. His flashlight lit up the dark area quite well. It would be slow going but there had to be something, some sort of clue, which would explain why the tunnel was in existence. He hadn't gone twenty feet when his flashlight started to grow dim. He hurried back the way he came and left the book shelf slight ajar as went in search of fresh batteries.

Mac checked all the usual places and no D batteries were anywhere to be found. Irritated but determined, he drove to the corner convenience store and bought a package. If Millie had been with him she would have had a fit over the price. Time was of the essence. He didn't want to waste a minute running to the big box store. With the Perrys in jail, the others would be heading home as soon as they returned from their outings. If Mac was correct, letting them go would be a huge mistake. His gut told him there was more to this story. Why would the Perrys go out of their way to make this murder look like the one previous? If they wanted to kill the old woman, they would have just murdered her and took off for heaven only knows where—right after the deed was done. He shook his head, doubt clouding his mind more than ever, and paid for his batteries.

He hurried home to the library. He paused upon entering the room. *I thought I left that doorway open. Huh. I must be losing it.* Mac opened the secret door and let himself through, his flashlight illuminating his path. He took his time. He sniffed the stale air. *Strange, smells like Millie's perfume.* Shining the light against the walls of the passage, looking for anything out of the ordinary. *There must be some sort of clue as to why this tunnel is here.*

He passed his one free hand over the rough walls as he walked. About halfway through the passage, he tripped over something. His flashlight went flying and everything went dark when the light bulb hit up against the stone wall. He broke his fall on something, no make that someone softer than he was. He pulled his phone out of his pocket so he could see who was lying on the floor. The familiar fragrance combined with the groan emanating from the unconscious form caused his stomach to turn. *Millie!*

Mac heard footsteps running in the opposite direction. There was nothing he could do. Millie's immediate needs took precedence over going after the guilty party.

Mac opened his phone, thankful for the little bit of light it lent. "Millie. Millie." She was moving her head slightly as moans still escaped her nearly still lips. "Millie, it's me, Mac. Honey." He tried to call out but had no signal that far underground. He hated to leave her but he didn't know how else to get help. "Honey, if you can hear me I'll be right back." He took off at a run. No more than two minutes later he was back by her side. "Help is on the way. I'm here."

Her eyes fluttered. When she saw Mac she closed them again and went limp.

"Millie, baby, stay with me. Come on. Open your eyes."

Sheriff Twiggs was the first on the scene followed closely by the EMT's. After securing Millie on the stretcher, Mac followed her through the tunnel—she to the waiting ambulance and he to Sheriff Twiggs truck. With the sirens blasting, Sheriff Twiggs followed going just as fast—with Mac in the passenger seat. If Mac could have, he would have pushed them to go faster.

Thankfully the hospital was only a few miles away.

Mac jumped out as they pulled Millie from the ambulance. He was by her side as they wheeled her in.

Her eyes fluttered open. "Mac."

"I'm right here, Sweetheart." He squeezed her hand and said goodbye with his eyes. He was left on the other side of the "Authorized Personnel Only" sign posted on the double doors. Sheriff Twiggs appeared with a cup of coffee and motioned for him to have a seat.

After signing the necessary papers, Mac joined the Sheriff. "What was I thinking?" He took the offered cup of coffee but didn't drink any. His mind was going back over what happened. "I knew something was wrong. I just knew it. And yet I left my wife in that house with a killer." He glanced at the man sitting next to him. "I'm losing my edge."

Sheriff Twiggs was quiet for a few seconds, his thoughts running deep. "I thought we had 'em Mac. I really did. Even got the Perrys true identities back late this morning. They're both wanted for murder. Seems we got a team for hire locked up in our jail cell. Course, they both denied having anything to do with Mrs. Santangelo. I didn't believe them." He rested his head in his hands. "I'm sorry I got you involved in this, Mac. I shoulda known better."

"You didn't get me involved. Whoever decided to murder a guest in our bed and breakfast decided that for us."

"Yeah, but I coulda took the fight elsewhere. Instead I thought we should keep our enemies close." He motioned to the double doors. "Now Millie's hurt. We gotta find this guy, Mac."

Neither man spoke.

Mac ran over everything that had happened thus far. He was missing something. They both were.

The doctor came through the doors and motioned for Mac who stood and met him halfway. "She's going to be fine. She's got herself a nice bump on the head and she's suffered a concussion. We want to keep her here overnight but if all the other tests come back negative she'll be heading home tomorrow morning. Best thing that can happen is she needs rest and she needs someone to keep an eye on her. My nurses will check in on her and watch that nothing comes of that head wound. She had a little bit of bleeding and we found a few particles in the wound."

Sheriff Twiggs interrupted. "I'd like to have those sent to my lab."

"I figured as much. We put them in an evidence bag and sealed it for you. I'll have my nurse bring it out." He turned to go. "Oh, and she's awake and asking for you. Just give us a few minutes to get her settled then someone will come get you." He returned the way he came.

Mac paced until a nurse called his name.

Chapter 12

Millie's head was throbbing. She rubbed the skin between her thumb and index finger. She couldn't remember who, but someone had told her that was a pressure point and could relieve headaches. She'd asked to hold off on her pain medication so she could see Mac without falling asleep mid-sentence. She was a light weight when it came to handling meds.

Her husband's voice announced his arrival. "Millie. Thank God you're OK."

"Well, my noggin' disagrees with you but hey, I'll live. Mac, Sheriff Twiggs arrested the wrong people. I'm sure of it."

"We've figured that much out. Not that those two are innocent. They're wanted by the FBI, CIA, and all the other three letter government organizations you can think of."

Millie paused. "For what?"

"They're hitmen. Work as a team. Although they denied having anything to do with this murder."

"You've got to be kidding me?"

"I wish I was. But no, they were hired to kill her but someone beat them to it. Sheriff didn't believe 'em." He smoothed her covers. "He does now."

Millie recognized Mac's behavior for what it was, nervous energy. She took his hands and made him look at her. "Mac, this isn't your fault." He tried to pull away but she held on tighter. "You're not listening to me. What happened isn't your fault."

It took a lot to bring tears to Mac's eyes. Seeing the bandages around his wife's head—knowing she could be a lot worse off—did the trick. "Millie, I don't know what I'd do without you. I should have been there. I should have this guy behind bars. This makes twice you've been assaulted. I…" He swallowed hard. "I'm gonna find out who did this. And when I do…"

"Mac, when you do you're going to let Sheriff Twiggs take care of them. Do you hear me? I need you too. I don't want to be visiting my husband with bars in-between us." She yawned. "Now, why don't you let the nurse know I'm ready for that pain pill. Go home and get some rest. I'll be safe here. I'm sure."

They both looked up when they heard Sheriff Twiggs clear his throat. "Darn tootin' you'll be all right. I've got my deputy sittin' right outside your door. He won't let anyone get past. Little lady, I promise we're gonna take good care of ya." He looked to Mac. "You've got my word."

Mac sat with Millie until she fell asleep then made the deputy take a bathroom break so he wouldn't have to leave her alone until relief came. He whispered, "I love you, Millie," before walking out the door.

Sheriff Twiggs was waiting in front of the hospital, truck running, ready to take Mac home. "You want to stop off for a cup of coffee before we head back? I reckon we could go over everything once more. Maybe somethin'll jump out at us."

"Yeah, I won't be able to sleep anyway. Might as well try and figure out who's going around trying to hurt my wife. And why. It's not like she knows anything."

Maybe it's just been wrong place wrong time."

"I don't know. I thought that with the shed but the tunnel? Seems to me someone could have easily hid in the shadows when they realized she was just looking for me. No, this has an intentional feel to it. Someone wants to hurt my wife. The question is, why?"

Chapter 13

Sunday morning Millie woke up worse off than when she'd gone to bed. Not even the pain pill could save her from Nurse Sam. That dude took his job seriously. Every two hours like clockwork he was checking her eyes, asking her questions. She was appreciative but darn, she could have used the extra sleep. She woke every two hours at home, for other reasons—OK, a weak bladder. There were times she wish she could just pee the bed. Now, when she could legitimately sleep, she wasn't allowed to sleep. She hated hospitals.

Lucy beat the breakfast tray by about 30 seconds. Which meant breakfast was going to taste a whole lot better than the alternative. She was surprised when the two women showed up to feed her. Velia was bearing the hospital's version of breakfast. She apologized but passed. Lucy's would be much tastier. Velia looked a little miffed but Millie ignored her. It wasn't as if it was personal, she didn't make the food herself. Velia was just delivering. Velia huffed a little then set the tray down for Millie's roommate and left to finish the patients' meal delivery rounds.

"I didn't know Velia worked here." She breathed in deeply as she opened the brown paper bag.

Lucy shrugged. "Yep, she's worked here for the last nine months or so. She enjoys it. The pay's not super high but she's got decent benefits."

Millie smiled at the tightly covered bowl of steel cut oats and the bag of goodies to mix in on her hospital tray. The lemon poppy seed muffin was still warm and the creamy butter melted instantly as she lathered it on the muffin. She took a bite then closed her eyes. "I can't believe how hungry I am. I slept through supper last night."

The mixed nuts and fruit, along with a little brown sugar, made oatmeal Millie's favorite breakfast. When she lived in the city, Starbucks provided. Now that the nearest Starbucks was in Green Bay, she relied on Lucy to provide. Which she did on occasion—special occasions. Apparently being bashed in the head qualified. Millie wasn't going to complain. She ate every morsel then sat back, content, sipping the hot coffee that came from the green thermos.

"Lucy, you are a Godsend. Truly. You knew just what I needed."

Lucy muttered flitting from one thought to the next. "Wandering around…getting bopped on the head… making us worry…"

"I'm sorry. I didn't mean to cause you any stress. I suppose you ended up having to go to the store after I said you wouldn't have to. Looks like the Perrys are not the culprits so the Sheriff wants everyone to remain. He's close to clearing all our guests. Which makes no sense. Someone has to be responsible."

Mac walked in as she finished her sentence. "Millie, you're supposed to be taking it easy. Not trying to solve a murder."

She stared him down. "Someone tried to off me. I'll have you know I fully intend to find this person and make sure our home becomes our sanctuary once more. I won't be afraid in my own home. I just won't." She picked up her coffee then abruptly set it down again, sloshing some steamy amber liquid over the side. "The doctor said I can go home once the nurse changes the dressing on my wound." She gave her husband an intense gaze. "And I plan on being proactive once I get there." Seeing the scowl on his face she added, "I can do a lot from my resting place in my bed."

"I'm glad mom and dad are still here. They can keep an eye on you when I'm gone."

"That's all I need."

"Well, that's the best I've got to offer. One of the kids would come in a heartbeat, but where would we put them?"

"Oh no, don't bother them. They have enough to worry about without adding me to the list."

He nodded. "Which is exactly why it's a good thing my parents are still here."

Millie reluctantly grunted her approval then mumbled, "I'd be just fine on my own."

Mac turned toward her. "What did you say?"

"Nothing."

"That's what I thought. Millie, don't you dare give me any grief about this. I can't be worrying about you and do what needs doing."

She knew he was right. Guilt spilled over from her growing up years and she hung her head in remorse. "Mac, I'm sorry to be so difficult. All those years you were on the force in the city and nothing ever happened. Now, we move north to a quiet little town by the bay and we have a murderer trying to take me out. I'm just not used to having my freedom taken away. I don't want you to worry about me, that's not my intent." She sheepishly raised her eyes to meet his. "I'll behave, I promise."

He sat down next to her on the bed and raised her hand to his lips and sighed. "No, you won't. But I know you'll try and that means a lot."

She grinned. "You know me too well."

Chapter 14

Mac's mom took to babysitting Millie so Mac went back to the tunnel. *Something has to be here.* This time he ran a long heavy duty extension cord and set up his bright shop lights. Between those and his flash light, He hoped he would find something useful. He slowly went over the cavernous walls, moving the lights as he went. His trained eye grazed every surface, slowly looking for clues, for anything that might reveal what was going on. A couple of hours later, and halfway through the tunnel, he found what he was looking for. A crude drawing of a woman holding a rose.

Even in its current state, the woman in the drawing looked nothing like Mrs. Hampton. He wondered if this was the woman who was killed so many years ago. Shining his light over a little showed another drawing of the woman lying down with the rose. Whoever drew these pictures had to have had a hand in the original death. Which means that poor woman was murdered too. Under the drawing there was a shelf with an empty glass bottle. The dust on the bottle had been disturbed. Mac hurried back to the library and called Sheriff Twiggs.

It wasn't long before the sheriff and one of his deputies joined Mac in the tunnel. The sheriff boomed, "And let there be light."

Mac chuckled. "Well, light does help one see in the darkness. Look what I found." He pointed to empty bottle lying on the natural shelf and the piece of artwork still visible in spite of the dampness.

"What do we have here?" He picked up the bottle with a gloved hand and turned it from side to side being careful not to touch it more than absolutely necessary. "And what is this?" He grinned at the nearly full fingerprint clearly visible by the naked eye then sobered. "Mac, you didn't touch this did you?"

"I think you know me better than that. I haven't disturbed a thing."

The grin returned to Sheriff Twigg's face. "We may have our first real piece of evidence here, Mac." He looked at his deputy. "Let's bag this and get it back to the office to run for fingerprints.

The deputy had finished taking pictures of the area then left with the one piece of evidence that could shine some light on the case. Both Mac and the Sheriff were optimistic about this being the turning point.

Mac stopped looking at the walls and turned toward the Sheriff. "Do you think we're looking at this from the wrong angle? Surely if the Perrys were hired to take out Mrs. Hampton and someone beat them to it, well, it might mean someone besides the mob was wanting her dead." He paused then continued, "Did you ever find her family?"

"I have one of the guys tracking down a couple of leads. He got a few names from the fish boil and we think we might have found them. We'll know more later this evening."

"Something else has been lurking at the back of my mind. Do you remember, when we were interested in buying this property, wasn't there someone else who was bidding too? I seem to remember someone getting pretty angry they didn't get the building."

"You know, now that you mention I seem to remember something about that."

"Yeah, and now that I'm thinking about it, we had some petty thefts and vandalism as we were getting this thing ready. Our contractor had several tools that went missing too. He chalked it up to employee theft, something he's dealt with before, or some local riffraff getting into trouble."

"You filed a police report, right?"

"Yep, we sure did."

"When we get out of this tunnel I'll call and have the guys pull the report. And I'll call the realty office and see who was bidding against you. It won't hurt to at least talk with them. You're right. We need to keep an open mind."

Chapter 15

Millie talked Patty into letting her go downstairs to visit for a while. She was tired of watching the television and staring at the same four walls. She concluded Patty was tired of her whining and relented just to shut her up.

Besides, she was getting hungry and the mush her mother-in-law tried to feed her wasn't doing it. She was bopped over the head. She didn't lose all her teeth. For heaven's sake. She could always count on Lucy to tempt her taste buds.

She slowly descended the stairs one step at a time, holding on to the handrail as she went. Pausing on the second floor, she heard whistling and popped her head in to see Velia dusting one of the guest rooms. Millie watched her work as she slowly ran her rag over the fireplace mantle. Millie looked on for a couple of minutes then backed out quietly so as not to disturb the young woman. She was impressed with Velia and her attention to detail. She seemed to take pride in her work.

Millie entered the kitchen feeling a bit weak and questioned her decision to make the trip. Her head was still hurting and she was a bit wobbly, but hunger and the need for conversation with someone other than Patty tipped the scales in favor of going down. She sat down at the kitchen table and waited for Lucy to come out of the pantry.

The mixer was on the counter along with butter. She was baking something. Perhaps for tomorrow's breakfast or maybe even cookies. She wasn't sure if Lucy was keeping up with everything. She was thankful Velia was helping her out. Millie felt bad she wasn't able to do her part.

Lucy jumped when she exited the pantry and nearly threw the ingredients she had piled up in her arms. "What are you doing down here? Mac is going to throw a tizzy fit."

"Lucy, we don't have to tell him, do we? I need some real food. Patty is trying to feed me baby food. At least that's what I think it is."

She put her hands on her hips and sighed. "Let me see what I've got." She opened the refrigerator and moved some things around, finally settling for a Tupperware container with a blue lid. "After you eat, I'm going to help you back up the stairs. I'll bring you some supper. I guess I thought Mac's mom would feed you." She opened the container slightly before putting it in the microwave.

Millie knew she was getting some homemade soup. She took one bite of the potato soup and decided the trip was completely worth it.

Lucy set a small plate with a thick piece of buttered bread next to her. "Lucy, what did I ever do without you?"

"I haven't the foggiest." She turned to face Millie. "Did you hear about your roommate from the hospital? She went in for a knee replacement surgery and came out dead. Who'd have thunk it?"

Millie stopped chewing and shook her head. "But, she was young and healthy. She hurt her knee playing tennis. What happened?"

Lucy shrugged her shoulders. "From what I heard, she had a heart attack. Strange things are happening in this town?" She shook her head. "I think you've gone and made the ghost mad."

Lucy kept talking but Millie couldn't hear a word of it over the whir of the blender. She would just smile and nod as if she heard her. Hopefully she hadn't agreed to anything she'd regret later, especially since the last words she heard had to do with an imaginary ghost.

Once she was finished eating she had just enough energy to make it back to her room. If she was lucky, Mac would be none the wiser. And she could only hope Patty wouldn't tell on her.

After a couple hour nap, Millie propped cushions behind her and sat in bed digging on her laptop. She searched for as much information as she could find on the house, who built it, liens held against it, permits obtained, public sale records, anything and everything she could think of and found nothing. She closed her laptop frustrated at the time spent with nothing to show for it.

Restless, she wandered around the apartment. Her in-laws were noticeably absent and the place was quiet. She made herself a cup of hot tea, then perched on her balcony and watched the sailboats in the bay. Soon the boats would all be stored making way for snow and ice. Still pretty to look at, but not nearly as much feasting for the eyes. Ice fishing and snowmobiling were regular activities on the smaller lakes in the area; the bay didn't freeze thick enough to allow for such activities.

Millie was thankful for the gas fireplace they'd added to their private quarters. The winter wind coming off the lake could send a chill through a person that would temper the hottest hot flash.

She was just about to go inside when she saw Mac getting into his truck. She yelled to him but he didn't hear her. A few minutes later, Lucy was booking it on foot, probably heading to the store. She said she would bring supper. Must have needed something. Millie watched her long grey pony tail swing back and forth. The little woman had more energy than Millie did at times. Even so,

Millie was surprised she didn't send Velia. It would be better use of her time to have the younger woman run errands. She'd have to talk to her about that. She didn't have to try and do everything herself. She yawned and decided another nap was in order.

Millie snuggled down into her covers. She heard a door close somewhere in the distance but her sleepy mind refused to contemplate who might be home. She just didn't have the energy.

Chapter 16

Mac parked at an angle in front of the real estate office. The sign on the door said the realtor would be back in fifteen minutes so he started glancing through the newspapers. All the business owners in town used those little plastic clock signs to step out for a few minutes. Darla probably needed a cup of coffee. Mac yawned. He could use one himself.

Not much caught his attention. He made comments as he glanced. The boy scouts were selling wreaths. He'd have to buy one this year for the front of the inn. A big one. A fifteen-year-old boy went missing and found several days curled up by a tree next to a bottle of tequila. The incident deemed an accidental alcohol poisoning and freezing temperatures. The last page yielded an article that had been mostly torn out. Mac could barely read the headline, "Woman missing from Mental Health Facility."

"Huh. Wonder…" His thinking out loud ended as Darla unlocked the reality office door.

He found himself continually thinking back to who was bidding against him for the bed and breakfast. If nothing more than to satisfy his own curiosity, he needed to know who it was. He paced in the lobby as he waited for Darla to be freed up.

She picked up the phone as soon as she walked in the door. He could hear her chatting on the phone. He didn't want to be rude and interrupt but at the same time, his burning question was more important than how badly Mrs. Elmer hit the high notes Sunday morning in church choir.

He paced in front of the door to make sure she saw him. A few minutes later, she stepped out of her office. "Mac, sorry to keep you waiting." She walked toward him and threw her arms around him. He'd never really known how to respond. "How are you?" She was a super huggy, touchy sort and if his stiff response gave her pause she never let on.

"I've been better."

"Oh, yeah, I've heard about all the trouble going on down at your place. It's all everyone's talking about. I mean, besides Mrs. Elmer in church Sunday. You missed it. I swear it sounded like someone trying to strangle a pigeon." She paused for a quick breath. "So, tell me what's been happening. You know how gossip goes, everything gets all mixed up and a person doesn't know what is what."

She perched her hand on her hip and cocked her head expectantly.

Mac knew from experience Darla could and would out talk him. Yet, if he wanted answers, he was going to have to give her something.

"Lucy keeps going on and on about this being the work of a ghost." He raised his eyebrows expecting her to agree with him. No matter how much he wanted to capitalize on the whole haunted inn experience, the very idea seemed absurd. He didn't really believe in ghosts.

"You do know the rumor about town, don't you? About neighbors seeing a long dressed figure moving about by candlelight through the darkened house?"

The alarm on his face caused her to continue. "This was before you moved in, of course. To my knowledge, she hasn't been seen since."

"What do you mean since we moved in? Um…was this going on when we were remodeling?"

"It was mostly happening before your offer was accepted. There were a couple of rumors of sightings after you bought the place, but those were questionable."

"As in someone trying to scare us off?"

"Yeah, I think so." She looked sheepish. "It wasn't me, I swear."

Mac scowled. "Who would do such a thing?"

Darla turned for her office. "Sheriff called. Said you needed to know who was bidding against you." She studied him for a moment. "I guess it's OK to hand these over to you. Since you're working for him and all." She waited as he glanced over the papers.

Mac studied the paperwork, not sure if he was seeing correctly. He looked to Darla for confirmation and she nodded.

He put the paperwork back in the large envelope. "Thanks a million, Darla. Maybe now we can figure out what's been happening."

"You don't think she had anything to do with it, do you?" Darla called after his retreating form.

"I don't know. But I'm sure gonna find out." He jogged toward his car and never heard her yell "I've already faxed this information over to the Sheriff."

***

Millie, still half asleep, answered the ringing phone and muttered, "Hello."

"Mrs. MacDonald? Um, I'm sorry to be bothering you, I know you're recuperating, but

Lucy asked me to give you a call. She is in a bit of trouble and needs your help."

Millie sat up a little straighter. "Lucy? What's happened? Is she OK?"

"The sheriff seems to think she's the cause of all the trouble that's been coming your way lately. She asked if you wouldn't mind coming down to the station to vouch for her. She could use her friends about now."

"Sure. Let me find a ride. I can't be driving. I'm still a bit out of it from the pain pills. They knock me out."

"Oh, I can come pick you up. It'd be no trouble at all."

Millie called out and heard nothing. "Well, I guess that's the only way I'm going to get there in a hurry. No one seems to be home."

"I'll be there in a few minutes. I'll see you soon."

Millie dialed Mac's phone but it went straight to voice mail. She shook her head and jotted a quick note and left it on the kitchen table.

She stepped outside at the same time a little brown hatchback pulled into the driveway. Velia waved and hopped out to help Millie in.

"Thank you, Mrs. MacDonald. I'm sorry for the inconvenience."

Millie patted Velia's arm as she sat down in the driver's seat. "It's OK. There are more important things than rest and Lucy is one of them. I can rest when I get back."

Velia drove a little faster than necessary. She pulled into an open parking spot in front of the station then hurried around to the passenger side door. "Here, let me help you." She practically carried Millie into the station. Millie was surprised at the girl's strength. "Mrs. MacDonald, we have to hurry. Lucy needs us."

"I'm sure Lucy is being treated fairly. Sheriff Twiggs is a good man." She was slightly dizzy and followed along the direction she was being pulled.

By the time Millie was seated in front of Sheriff Twiggs she was close to passing out.

The sheriff pulled his toothpick out of his mouth. "Why, Mrs. MacDonald, what are you doing out? Your husband is going to have my hide."

"Velia was supremely worried about Lucy. Have you arrested her? What happened?" She closed her eyes and took a deep breath.

He chuckled. "No, I didn't arrest her. I wanted to ask her a few questions dating back to when you were bidding on the house. Seems Lucy was bidding against you."

Millie opened her eyes. "I didn't know that. She never said a word."

"Well, she sure was. Darla over at the real estate company kept a real tight lid on it. Seems Lucy didn't want people knowing she was going after the old inn."

Millie was confused. She wasn't sure if the drugs were causing her confusion but she was having a hard time drawing parallels to their current situation. "What does that have to do with now?"

"Well, maybe nothing. Then again, maybe everything. The neighbors spotted ghosts in the house during that time but they never saw anyone coming or going from any of the doors. My gut tells me whoever was responsible for the apparitions knew about the secret tunnel. And if the ghosts were meant to scare you away— perhaps the same ones responsible back then are responsible now. Which puts Lucy in the hot seat." He paused. "She had the most to gain if you backed down."

"But, Lucy would never—I mean, she's part of the family." She looked at the Sheriff. "I can't believe she would purposefully hurt me."

Sheriff Twiggs shrugged his shoulders. "That's what I am to find out."

Millie's face flushed. She turned to Velia. "Can you find me a bottle of water? Please?"

The young woman nodded then stood up.

"There's water in the fridge in the kitchen. Down the hall on the right."

Velia left the room for the kitchen so Millie stood up and said, "Is Lucy still here? Can I talk with her?"

He shook his head. "She's here but I don't think that's a good idea. First, I don't want you stressing yourself out. She isn't under arrest but I want her to sit tight for a little bit—just give her a little time to stew. Maybe she'll think of something that can help us." He stood as well. "Why don't you go home and rest. We'll figure this out and get things back to normal."

"My cook is being held for questioning, I have a houseful of guests, and my head is spinning. I think I may have to put Mac's parents to work." Velia came in and handed Millie the open water bottle.

She took a long drink. "Thank you, Velia. The sheriff is going to chat a little longer with Lucy but she'll be home before too long. Why don't we head back to the inn? I'm worn out."

Velia didn't look pleased about the outcome but she did as she was told. Millie climbed into the passenger seat and Velia drove away as the Sheriff waved them off.

Chapter 17

Mac read the note for the third time then tried her cellphone, also for the third time getting her voice mail. "Mill, where are you?"

He called the sheriff. "Hey, it's Mac. I need to talk to you. Has Darla got those reports to you yet?"

"She sure did. I've been meaning to call you too. I just released Lucy. I didn't much like her answers but I don't have anything on her."

Mac sighed. "Millie's gone missing."

"She was here a little while ago. Seems Lucy's niece thought Millie could talk me out of holding her aunt." He paused. "She should have been home by now. I wonder if they stopped off somewhere."

"I'm not liking this."

"Me either. I'll be right over."

Mac hung up and ran to the window when he heard a car door slam. "Lucy!" He opened the door for her. "Have you heard from Velia or Millie?"

She grunted. "I have stuff to do. Sheriff taking me to the station for nothin'. Yeah, I was bidding against ya, but that don't mean I killed nobody. Good grief. A woman can't be tryin' to buy her a business these days without somebody thinkin' she's a murderer." She huffed her way to the kitchen.

Mac tried again, this time a little louder. "Lucy! Have you seen or heard from Velia or Millie?"

She stopped. "No, I haven't. I asked that young lady to bring you or Millie to the station to vouch for me. Nobody showed up."

"Velia took Millie to the station, Lucy. But they haven't returned. Do you know where they might have gone?"

"Oh. I didn't think they came. Why didn't the Sheriff say somethin'?"

"Lucy!"

She shook her head. "Velia lives with me, or at least she sleeps there. Maybe Millie wasn't feeling too good, Mac. Maybe she took her back to the hospital. Velia working there and all she'd know if Millie needed help."

Mac called the hospital. No sign of either Millie, or Velia, who failed to show up for a shift delivering lunches to patients.

Lucy began pacing. "Mac, I know I didn't tell you about me wanting the inn, but you have to believe me, I would never hurt Millie. I'm not even sore about you two getting it. I'm actually glad. I never would have had enough money to get this old building fixed up proper. And what bank would have loaned it to me? Not a one."

She picked up the house phone and dialed out then shook her head and replaced the handset. "She's not answering her phone."

Another door slam sent Mac running for the front door. "Sheriff. I thought you might be Millie." He turned back for the kitchen and Lucy who was talking into the receiver.

"Did you reach them?"

"I left her a voice mail. She'll be calling me back soon. I'm sure of it."

The sheriff caught Mac's eye and motioned for him to follow him.

"What do you got?"

"When Lucy was in questioning, we asked her about her niece."

Mac interrupted. "Yeah, we know she's not really her niece."

The sheriff was annoyed. "Let me finish, will ya? I already know that too." He scowled but continued. "Velia is an escapee from the Brown County Psychiatric Hospital."

"What?" Mac sputtered. "The psychiatric hospital?"

Sheriff Twiggs nodded.

"Yeah, she went missing nearly a year and a half ago. Guess since she called Lucy her aunt no one really gave her any thought."

"She was working at the…" Mac paced. "…she was serving people their food at the hospital. Didn't anyone do a background check on the woman?"

Sheriff shrugged. "Seems she started off volunteering. The hospital was just happy to get someone to help out. Then she did such a good job, well, she knew her way around a hospital so well, they hired her on. Mac, they had no idea she knew hospitals so well because she lived in one, honest."

"She's got Millie, Twiggs. She's got my wife." He stared out the window. "What was she in for? What did she do?"

"Well, that's where things get a bit hairy. Her doctor is on her way here now. She says we are not to approach Velia, it will only make matters worse." He glanced at his watch. "She should be here…well, in the next fifteen minutes."

"Sheriff, I need to know what she was in there for."

He shook his head. "I don't have the whole picture. Dr. Morgan is going to explain everything to us when she gets here. Fifteen minutes, Mac. I promise, no more."

Mac's Irish temper was about to get the best of him. "Did you put out an APB on her car?"

Sheriff Twiggs nodded. "We've got men searching for them now. State patrol too. And the next county over. Everyone's looking, Mac, We'll find them."

Ten minutes later, two vehicles pulled up in front of the bed and breakfast. A petite woman with spikey blond hair, and what looked like two body guards, exited the vehicles and hurried to the front door. Mac had the door open before they could knock.

"Dr. Morgan?"

She nodded then entered the foyer. "This is Ben and Jack." She turned to the sheriff. "Have you found her yet?"

He shook his head. "We've got a lot of country, a lot of woods."

Lucy sheepishly entered the room. "I think I might know where they are."

Mac ran to her and took by the shoulders.

The sheriff intervened. "Mac, let's hear her out."

"Well, sometimes she goes to the lake to think. There's a fishing shanty that's been abandoned. She fixed it up a little and she spends a lot of time there—when she's not with me, that is. She likes to fish off the dock and well, she likes the sound of the water."

"Where is it? Do you know?"

Lucy nodded. "I can show you."

Dr. Morgan addressed the small group. "It's important that no one act rashly. She's probably confused and interweaving her past with her present. No one…" She looked at Mac, "…do anything to scare her. I need her thinking as clearly as possible. Lucy, she's attached herself to you. This is a good thing. I'm going to need you nearby so she can see you're OK. Do not show disapproval in her, no matter what happens. Her mother was extremely abusive and she needs to know she is safe with you." She addressed the group again. "Is there any reason why she would see Mrs. MacDonald as a threat to Lucy?"

They quickly explained the sale of the house but the doctor shook her head. "No, it's got to be something more personal…something she strongly believes in and sees Mrs. MacDonald threatening."

Lucy gasped. "Surely it can't be the ghosts."

The doctor narrowed her eyes.

Lucy explained her theory that the house was haunted. She told them she'd started the rumor to hopefully scare away any possible house buyers and to bring down the asking price. She didn't really think Velia believed her. It became something of a game, she thought, to both of them. "Apparently it was more than a game to Velia."

Dr. Morgan asked, "And Mrs. MacDonald was vocal in her disagreement?"

Mac nodded. "I played along, thinking it might bring us more business. If I hadn't of...maybe this wouldn't have happened."

The sheriff offered his own bit of advice. "No sense second guessing an unstable woman. Sane women are hard enough to predict."

Mac had his keys in hand. "Can we go now? Every minute that passes increases the chance she will hurt my wife."

Dr. Morgan nodded. "Remember, Lucy and I'll do the talking. She knows both of us and she isn't afraid of us. That is really important."

Lucy led them to a wooded area near the shore of the bay. They found the brown hatchback parked in the clearing. Between the four vehicles, they boxed the car in then proceeded quietly on foot, with Lucy leading the way. She pointed to a small shanty with a dim light shining from beneath the door.

"That's it." She whispered.

The sheriff pulled his handgun. Dr. Morgan touched his arm and shook her head. She motioned for everyone but her and Lucy to stand back then she approached the door and knocked. She heard shuffling inside the small building.

"Velia, it's me, Dr. Morgan. Lucy is with me. Will you open the door?"

A small voice sounded from the other side of the door. "Aunt Lucy?"

Dr. Morgan nodded to Lucy.

"It's me, Velia. I thought I'd come by and see how you are faring in your little house. Did you get the decoratin' all done?"

The door slightly creaked open. "Can you come back tomorrow, Aunt Lucy. I kinda have company."

"Oh, who's visitin' ya at this hour? It's already getting' dark."

"Well, it's a surprise I've been working on for you. I don't want to spoil your surprise. Why don't you go on home? I'll show you tomorrow, I promise."

Lucy looked to Dr. Morgan in a panic. She was trying to get Velia's guard down but it wasn't working. "Velia, can I have some water. I'm getting mighty thirsty out here."

"Lucy, go on home. We'll talk tomorrow."

Dr. Morgan spoke. "Velia, I need to know if Mrs. MacDonald is OK. Is she your visitor?"

The question was met with silence then the door flew open. "Now you've done it. You've gone and ruined the surprise."

Ben and Jack had been waiting patiently on either side of the door for their opportunity to grab Velia. She stomped out of the little shack to confront Dr. Morgan and was flanked by a pair of strong hands.

The small bundle went ballistic. She had more strength than any man Mac knew. As soon as she was secure, he ran into the shack and looked around. Millie was unconscious heaped in a corner. The EMT's loaded her up as Mac and the Sheriff searched the small room. They found a small bag of some sort of chemical which they sent with the EMT's. For the second time in a matter of days, Mac sat in the passenger side of the Sheriff's truck, lights on, following his wife to the hospital. Twice was enough for a lifetime.

Chapter 18

Mac held Millie's hand and waited for her to wake up. Mac couldn't wait to see her smile. He rested his eyes in the chair next to her bed after hearing she was only given a sleeping pill. Combined with her pain medications, she was pretty much out of it, which was the only reason she was alive.

The substance found at the shanty was potassium chloride, the same chemical used to kill Mrs. Hampton. He heard Millie stirring.

"Mac." She looked around the room. "What am I doing here?"

"You don't remember what happened?"

"No, the last thing I remember was being at the police station with Velia. Is she OK? Did we have an accident?"

"No, this was no accident. She slipped you a sleeping pill somehow then took you to a little shanty on the lake."

"Why on earth would she do something like that?"

"I'm not exactly sure yet. Sheriff dropped me off here so I could make sure you're all right. He's with her now, trying to figure out what happened."

"Mac, I'm fine. Obviously. Go! Make sure this nightmare if over."

He kissed her hand. "Are you sure?"

"Mac!"

"OK, OK, I'm going. Get some rest though. When you wake up I'll be here."

She yawned. "Great minds." Her eyes slowly closed as he quietly crept out of the room.

Mac called Uber for a ride and told the driver he'd give him a fifty if he stepped on it—and he'd pay the ticket if they got pulled over.

The kid driving raised his eyebrows and stepped on the gas, sending Mac's head to the headrest. Five minutes later, they skidded to a stop in front of the police station. Mac threw some cash at the kid and ran for the door. Out of breath, he asked, "Where's the Sheriff?"

The receptionist responded, "He's in the interrogation room."

Mac knew the way. He stopped by the kitchen for a bottle of water, his throat was dry from panting. He arrived at the observation room and looked through the one way glass to see Dr. Morgan seated next to Velia.

Sheriff Twiggs was listening in and nodded in his direction. "Millie OK?"

"Yeah. She'll be fine. I miss anything?"

The sheriff shook his head. "Nope. We're just getting started. Should be an interesting story, to say the least. This case was a doozy."

"Sure was. I'm ready for it to be over." Both men grew quiet when they heard Dr. Morgan speak up.

"Velia, can you tell me what happened? Why did you have Mrs. MacDonald in your little apartment?"

"She didn't believe Aunt Lucy. She should have believed her—that Mrs. Hampton was killed by a ghost."

"But, she wasn't killed by a ghost, was she, Velia?"

Velia looked up. "The other woman was. I saw the pictures on the wall in the tunnel."

"What about Mrs. Hampton?"

"Aunt Lucy said something bad would happen. I wanted to make her happy. Something bad had to happen."

"What did you do?"

"I got some sleeping pills from the hospital. Same as the one I gave Mrs. MacDonald. I crushed up the pill and put it in her water. When Mrs. Hampton was sleeping, I gave her potassium chloride. Everybody believed Aunt Lucy after that, everyone but Mrs. MacDonald. She still didn't believe her. I needed to protect Aunt Lucy.

So, I gave Mrs. MacDonald a sleeping pill too. Only thing is, I didn't have another syringe. If I'd gone to the hospital I could have got one. So I was going to put it in her water but she wouldn't wake up. She kept sleeping."

Dr. Morgan continued. "How did you know about the woman from a hundred years ago?"

"In the tunnel. There's a whole bunch of drawings. Some in the middle of the tunnel, some at the end, by the little hideout."

Mac looked at the Sheriff and raised his eyebrows. He hadn't made it that far in his examination of the tunnel. Once this was settled he'd have another go at the secret tunnel—see what other secrets it was concealing.

The doctor continued. "How did you know about the tunnel?"

"I found it one day by accident. I was looking around the shed and found those old newspapers. When I looked down I saw my picture then ripped it out..." She smiled, proud of her quick thinking. "...and I didn't want anyone to see it. So they wouldn't recognize me." Velia rested her hands on her lap. "I went to move the papers and I tripped over something. When I looked closer, I saw it was a door. A secret door." Her eyes lit up. That's when I found the secret passageway. Then I found the blueprints down in the tunnel. Somebody hid 'em on the little shelf down there. But I found 'em and put up on my wall. With my picture."

"Was there a reason you chose Mrs. Hampton to die?"

Velia cocked her head. "She reminded me a little bit of the woman in the tunnel pictures. So I chose her. And she was in the same bedroom. So, it was a sign."

Sheriff Twiggs shook his head. "The woman has the whole mob on her tail and an escaped psych patient is the one to do her in. Where's the irony in that?"

Mac grimaced. "You know, I found that article she's talking about in those newspapers I kept. Only thing was, most of it was torn out then I got interrupted and forgot all about it." He looked at the sheriff. "The clipping was on her shanty wall, huh?"

"Yeah, that and the blue prints, the missing tools from the construction site, and a picture of Lucy with a necklace Lucy said went missing. She thought she'd just misplaced it. Velia had it set up as a little shrine to her hero. Guess she didn't lose it. Kind of creeps me out."

Mac involuntarily shuddered.

Ed and Jack were inside the room with Dr. Morgan. Both were silent and motionless. When Dr. Morgan joined Mac and the Sheriff in the observation room, one of the big guys stood in front of the door. The small police station didn't exactly have state of the art escape proof chambers.

"I would like to take her back to Brown County Psychiatric Hospital. When she goes to court we'll bring her back up here. I will tell you we'll push for an insanity plea. She isn't in touch with reality. At a young age she watched a man beat her mother to death. Her instinct is to protect any woman she sees in a motherly role. To her, her Aunt Lucy was in danger. Her mind is incapable of thinking through situations and coming to reasonable deductions. No court in this country would sentence her to jail time. I can guarantee that."

Sheriff Twiggs and Dr. Morgan signed the necessary paperwork for Velia to be transferred back to the high security hospital. "You'll be sure to keep track of her this time, won't you?"

Dr. Morgan nodded. "As long as Velia is living stress free, she can seem as normal as you and I." She tightened her lips. "As you have already experienced. She managed to get a job here, didn't she?" She paused then added, "One of the aids went against protocol and well, let's just say she isn't working for the hospital any longer."

Mac watched the two goons walk Velia to the van. Dr. Morgan drove herself and both vehicles pulled out of the parking lot and headed south. He looked at the Sheriff. "So, that's it then?"

"Guess so. You know better than I do, Mac. You don't always get the feel good ending. Not every case is cut and dried." He paused. "You going back to the hospital tonight?"

"Yeah. I think they're going to let Millie come home tonight. She was only sleeping off a sleeping pill, nothing more. Now, if she'd woken up we'd be having another discussion altogether. I've never been more glad pain pills knock her out. Combined with that sleeping pill, she was out for hours."

"Well, why don't you go back and take your wife home. I'll come by in the morning and update you on everything else I've found out in the past 24 hours."

Mac shook the sheriff's hand. "Thanks much. I'll see you tomorrow." He started to walk away then turned back. "You wouldn't by chance be going out for anything, are you?"

"You need a ride, don't you?"

"Yeah. Back to the inn if it's OK with you. I spent every dime I had on me to get here from the hospital and I'm going to need a vehicle to bring Millie home in."

Sheriff Twiggs laughed. "Come on. I'll take you home."

***

Millie talked the doctor into letting her go home. She wanted to spend the night curled up next to her husband. As they approached their front door, they heard the television blasting and Patty's voice trying to be heard over the sound.

"Pat, do you want a sandwich? I said, do you want a sandwich?"

Mac and Millie paused and listened.

"I'm sure Millie has something in this fridge to eat. Where in the world did they go? Just when you need that girl…"

Mac pulled Millie to him and whispered. "I have an idea." He led her down the stairs to the Fish Suite. "Do you think you can handle being in this room?"

She smiled. "Does it mean I get you all to myself?"

"That's exactly what it means."

She kissed him in reply. "It's been cleaned and is ready for our next guests. This is a great idea, Mac."

He took out his master key and opened the door. The light above the fish tank was glowing, a fire was already lit, and a plate of cheese and crackers were sitting on the bureau.

"Mac McDonald. You already had this planned, didn't you?"

"Mmhmm. I stopped by to get the car and thought we both could use some quiet time." He led her in the room. "Want a snack? I have juice and hot tea. Sound good?"

She smiled and sunk down in the luxurious arm chair in front of the fire. "We sure do know how to treat our guests, don't we?"

Mac sat down in a matching chair and put his feet on the ottoman. "We sure do."

Chapter 19

Sheriff Twiggs sat at the dining room table and officially told everyone they could go home, including Pat and Patty who changed their minds and thought they might stay on for a few more days. The weather was supposed to be beautiful and after talking to the newlyweds, they decided they had to go on a lighthouse tour. Millie groaned when she heard their plans. She murmured to Mac, "At least we have an empty room for them now. We'll put them in the Fish Suite once it's cleaned up."

He grinned. "I'll move their things as soon as we're done here."

She nodded.

After all the guests left to pack, Sheriff Twiggs told them the rest of the story.

"Velia tried to poison you at the hospital. She added potassium chloride to your breakfast tray. Lucy saved your life."

Millie's face turned ashen. "My roommate. Oh no!"

The sheriff nodded his head. "Yeah, another victim in this strange woman's saga. It's sad."

Millie dabbed her eyes. "Will you get me her information? I'd like to send her family a card, flowers, something."

He nodded then went on. "It appears the harbor patrol found the body of Mr. Santangelo. He was tied to a block of cement, exactly where Mr. and Mrs. Perry said he would be, about 15 fifteen feet under water. The hitmen…is that how you say that? Is she called a hitman or a hitwoman?" He looked to Mac who shrugged his shoulders. "Anyway, they are being extradited back to Illinois. They're wanted all over the world. Since they didn't commit a crime here, well, technically I guess they did steal your boat. I suppose murder trumps theft. By the way, they did apologize profusely and said they would make sure your boat is replaced. Apparently, they have their standards.

"Mr. Normal is on his way back to Chicago ready to pay out both Mr. and Mrs. Santangelo's life insurance policies. We found her family. Eleanor Cooper was the young woman you saw with the three boys. Apparently Mrs. Santangelo left everything to that little family. They are in quite the state of shock. I introduced them to Mr. Normal and the poor woman nearly fainted when she heard how much she would be inheriting. She can even hire a nanny now to help if she wants to.

"Mr. Phillips put in an offer on a resort not too far from here and his offer was declined. He failed to counter and decided perhaps he didn't want to be in the resort business after all. I have my suspicions about him, but, I had to cut him loose. He took off for Chicago complaining about country folks. I guess city life is more for him. I think the guy's bad news but a bad feeling won't hold up in court.

"That leaves the newlyweds. The only ones who are exactly who they said they were. He'll be starting work tomorrow at his father-in-law's sporting goods store and she will be setting up their home." He sighed and stood up. "Lucy feels horrible about everything that happened. Besides the harmless prank of saying the inn was haunted, she had no part in anything Velia did. She didn't even know the gal was taking tools and showing up as a ghost at night. I'll get going. She wants to talk to you alone." He tipped his hat. "I'm sure glad you're OK, Mrs. MacDonald." He left through the front door.

Lucy was standing at the entry way. "I'm sure sorry about all the trouble I've caused you two." She approached them then held out her hand. "Here's my notice. I've enjoyed workin' for you." She turned to walk away.

Millie watched the feisty woman turn away. "Lucy, please don't go yet."

Lucy stopped and slowly turned back around then grimaced. "I know you're mad at me. I'd be mad too. Go ahead. I can handle it." She closed her eyes tight and tightened her fists by her side.

"Lucy, I'm not mad at you. At least not yet. If you go through with this notice, then I'll for certain be mad. How am I supposed to run this place without you?"

Lucy opened her eyes in surprise. "You mean, you don't want me to go?"

"No, Ma'am. I don't. In fact, I want you to help us think of some good ghost stories to put on the website. If we're going to use this haunted house story to our advantage, we're going to need all the help we can get. Besides, do you think Mac is going to help me in the kitchen?"

All three laughed. Word was already spreading and the reservations were already pouring in.

Mac carried his parents' luggage to the Fish Suite. Pat and Patty were excited to be moving to a comfortable guest room, until they saw it was the room the poor woman died in.

Patty threw a bit of a fit. "You can't expect us to stay in this room. Why, I just couldn't."

Mac stopped and looked at his mother. "Why not? Millie and I stayed in here last night and we're fine. It's really a nice suite. You'll love it."

He started to carry the luggage in when his father stopped him. "Son, why don't you carry that luggage on to the car? I think we're gonna head on home. We'll come back up next spring and do the lighthouse tour.

Mac grinned as he picked up the suitcases. He figured as much.

Chapter 20

Mac slowed the boat down and dropped the anchor once he hit his "hot" spot for fishing. Millie balked at coming along but secretly she enjoyed being out on the boat with Mac. She brought a picnic lunch, a thermos of hot coffee, and a good book—Agatha Christie's *And Then There Were None*— in case the fishing wasn't any good.

He ran his hand against the new boat. It was bigger and had more gadgets than his old one. If he had been an official member of the police force he never would have been able to accept this beauty. He still felt a little bit of guilt when he took the time to think about it. He decided the money used on the boat was earned legitimately and not blood money.

Every time he discussed it, Millie just shook her head. "Just be thankful you got your boat back," She would tell him if he started to complain.

She was pouring two cups of hot coffee when Mac sat down beside her. "Are the poles ready?"

"No, not yet. I want to talk to you for a minute." He cozied up next to her.

"Mac, what is up?"

"Can't a guy just want to sit close to his wife?"

"Mac, we're on a fishing boat. We have bait. I know I can't compete with that. Now, I'll ask again. What do you want?"

He harrumphed. "Fine. Sheriff Twiggs asked me if I want to work part time for him." He looked at her with pleading eyes. "Can I?"

"Mac MacDonald! Since when do you have to ask my permission to do anything?"

"Woman, do you think I'm stupid? I know I don't have to ask permission. But, I do want to eat again. And sleep next to you. And wake up the next morning. So, can I?"

She threw her head back and laughed. "How did I know that was coming? I figured as much. Besides, we've encountered more danger since you've been retired. I think we were safer when you were working.

Mac grinned and pulled out a fat, juicy worm. He baited his hook and cast. Millie sipped her coffee and began reading her book.

PLEASE ENJOY THIS EXCERPT FROM BOOK 2 OF THE BROTHER BAY COZY MYSTERY SERIES

CATCH & RELEASE

Chapter 1

Mac rubbed his stomach then leaned back in his chair. "Dang, that was good." He'd found his new favorite hangout, Two Doors Down. In Chicago, where he worked as a detective for 30 years, the cops had a coffee shop where they'd congregate, have pie, and chew the fat. Now that he was working part time for the Brother's Bay, Door County, Wisconsin Sheriff's office, Mac felt at home.

Sheriff Twiggs grunted in agreement then took a long draw on his steaming coffee. Both men watched the snow swirl in little gusts through the big picture window facing Main Street.

"I think we got us a blizzard about to hit."

"Looks like." The sheriff twirled his toothpick.

"Think they're gonna cancel?"

"Nope. Ain't happened yet. That's why we've got parkas and shanties. Ice fishin' ain't for girlies."

Mac raised his eyebrows. "Better not let my wife hear you say that."

"I won't."

The Sheriff was the most relaxed lawman Mac had ever met. Good stock. Just what was needed for a man in his position. "Do we get to do any fishin'?"

Sheriff Twiggs nodded. "As long as there ain't no trouble. I caught a record Walleye last year. Got me a blue ribbon and everything. It's hangin' above my fireplace. You and missus will have to come over after the contest and have some supper."

The sheriff lost him on the word Walleye. Mac felt his blood stir. Fishing had to be his favorite thing to do. "What'd you say?"

"I said you'll have to come over for some of that fish we'll fry up after the weekend."

Mac's eyes perked up. "Tell us what to bring. We'll be there."

The Open Door was a cross between northern woods and artsy-fartsy, a little more than one of the other, depending on who you asked and what time of year you did the asking.

The door flew open and slammed against the wall. Peter Godding stomped across the rug without paying attention to the state of his boots. The wrath of Liza Simms, proprietor of The Open Door, would descend on anyone who didn't at least attempt to clean their feet. Mostly locals graced the doors after Christmas and before May so Liza could let her temper flare a little. Summer was a different story—she had to play nice.

The sheriff raised his hand. "Peter, over here."

The linebacker lookalike acknowledged him with a nod of his head then clunked his way toward the occupied table.

Mac noticed the dirty look Liza shot Peter's way then dismissed it when he saw the muddy ice trail he was leaving behind him as he walked. He made a mental note to bring a towel to dry his boots off next time he stopped at The Open Door for a bite.

Mac had only been in Peter's presence once since moving to Brother Bay and the situation was more of a passing one another in the throes of business rather than down time to actually get to know one another. Mac was looking forward to meeting the sportsman. He was a legend in competition fishing. His love of the sport launched his sporting goods store—with which

Mac was very well acquainted—per his bank account.

Mac rose and shook the man's hand. "Mac MacDonald."

Peter barely acknowledged Mac's introduction, which bristled, a little.

"Sheriff, you've got to do something about Brady. He keeps moving my shanty and I swear, if you don't do something, I will."

"Woah, settle down. Take a load off." Sheriff Twiggs nodded toward the chair adjacent then waited for Peter to follow instructions. "Now, tell me what's happened."

The rivalry between Brady and Peter dated back to high school, though neither of them would admit it. Both had their eye on the same girl, both blamed each other when she died in a car accident after partying a little too hard. North woods kids loved to drink. Playing doctor and drinking—got em' into a whole heap a trouble.

Brady Simmons owned the most successful charter fishing company in Door County. He made a point to order all his needed items from online suppliers. He refused to spend a dime of his hard-earned money to line Peter Godding's pocket—even if he did provide jobs for 30 plus Door County residents.

Liza slammed a cup of coffee down on the table—sloshing the rich brew over the sides and onto the saucer in the process—in front of Peter. He didn't bother to look at her but picked up the cup and took a long drink. "You still make a mean cup of coffee, Liza."

She stomped off and he started laughing. "That little gal can still make me laugh."

Mac thought to himself, my wife would not like this guy.

"So, what are you gonna do, Sheriff?"

Sheriff Twiggs sighed. "I'll talk to him. Get him to see reason."

The door opened once again sending in a blast of arctic freeze and a flurry of cold white stuff. Mac heard an expletive escape Peter Godding's mouth.

"Speak of the devil." He stood up to intimidate his nemesis. "Moving shanties around on the ice makes a person cold. Here to warm up?"

Brady shook his head, ignored the intentional goading, and sat on a stool at the counter. Mac liked his style a lot better than the lug next to him.

Liza poured the fisherman a cup of coffee then glared at Brady.

Mac wondered what was up between the café owner and Peter. A messed-up floor wouldn't cause a grudge to be carried out this long, not even in the meanest spirited woman. Liza may have a tough demeanor, but she wasn't mean. *Hmmm…*

Brady ignored the sheriff and sauntered to the counter.

Liza marched around to the dining area and hopped on a chair. She stood 5 foot 1 on a good day. "Brady Godding, if you even think you're gonna start something in my diner I'll have you thrown out and banned, do you hear me?"

He grunted in response and kept advancing.

"Oh no you're not." She jumped down as Brady stood and turned around.

"You want something, Godding?"

Mac compared the two men. Peter Godding was bigger, no doubt. But he'd let himself go somewhat. He carried as much flab as he did muscle. Simmons on the other hand, was pure muscle. His arms were bulging at rest and the muscles in his neck were taut. The man's job was physical. He was still a hands-on type business owner. Either man could win in a match up—if it came to blows.

Everything happened with seconds so Mac had a hard time keeping up. The sheriff, approaching from behind Godding, was hidden by the large man's girth. Godding, shoved Brady who reared back with a fist and delivered as Godding ducked. The result—Sheriff Twiggs with a bloody nose. The whole place grew still. The only sound was a unison intake of air from nearly 20 patrons and one loud gasp from Liza, the café owner, who ran to Sheriff Twiggs with a cloth.

Not even a bloody nosed fazed the sheriff. He picked up his phone, called a deputy then took the two men into the station and booked them both into cells opposite one another.

Godding was the first to complain. "Sheriff, what are you booking me for? I wasn't the one to hit you."

Sheriff nodded. "You started this mess. If you had kept your mouth shut and let me handle it you wouldn't be there. You had to get up and do your thing. Now, you'll be spendin' some time in here coolin' your heels."

Godding smirked. "I want to call my lawyer."

Sheriff picked up the house phone. "Well, looks like you'll be waitin' a bit. Phones are down."

Peter Godding hit the wall then leered into Brady's cell before sinking down on the cot. "You'll pay for this, do you hear?"

Brady was already lying down on his own cot and didn't respond.

Mac grinned as he poured himself a cup of coffee then asked quietly, "Are you going to book them?"

The sheriff removed his toothpick. "Nah, I'll spring em' here in an hour or two. Give em' a chance to catch their breath."

Mac laughed. "I bet that'll be the last time they pull a stunt like that."

The sheriff raised his eyebrows. "I don't know what gave you that idea. These two have been guests of the Brother Bay Jail more times than I can count. And every time they've checked in together."

He leaned back and rested his boots on his scratched up wooden desk. "You pour me a cup while you were in there?"

Mac disappeared for another cup.

A few hours later, Sheriff Twiggs rattled the keys. "You boys best get on home. The weather's getting' bad at there. Think you can stay out of trouble?"

Both men grunted in response and disappeared before the sheriff could change his mind.

"You better head on home too, Mac. No sense in both of us sticking it out here."

By midnight a person couldn't see a foot in front of them. Mac was in a sweat suit under two blankets and a down comforter still shivering. Millie was snoring, a little drool escaping her mouth with nothing but the sheet on. He just shook his head then threw another log on the fire. He shivered a little harder just looking at her. "Brrr…" he mumbled quietly then climbed back into bed. As soon as he was snuggled in, the cellphone rang. Millie stirred but didn't wake up. *Who in heaven's name is calling at this hour?* He pulled one hand out of the burrow he'd made himself and answered quietly. "Hello."

The sheriff was at the other end. He listened intently then offered to come in. "Okay, well, if you're sure."

He set his phone on the end table.

Millie asked, "Who was that?"

"The Sheriff. Go back to sleep."

Her eyes opened slightly. "What'd he want?"

"Apparently, Peter Godding didn't make it home last night. His girlfriend called the Sheriff's office looking for him."

"Okay." She slipped back into slumber land, her lips slightly parted.

For once, Mac had a harder time of it. He couldn't help but wonder. *Where in the world did Peter Godding go?*

Recipes for In-laws & Outlaws

Breakfast Casserole

7 slices cubed bread
½ lb shredded Swiss cheese
1 lb cubed ham, sautéed slightly to remove any water
½ chopped sautéed onion
8 ounces sautéed mushrooms
3 eggs
2 cups whole milk
½ tsp salt
¼ tsp dry mustard
½ stick butter

Place cubes of bread from five slices in a 9x12 greased pan. Arrange, cheese, ham, onion, and mushrooms over bread.

In a separate bowl beat eggs, milk, salt, and dry mustard. Pour over bread mixture in 9x12 pan.

Melt butter and toss remainder of bread cube to coat. Sprinkle of top of casserole.

Refrigerate overnight.

Bake at 325 degrees for one hour.

Lucy's French Toast

3 large eggs
1 cup half-and-half
Pinch of salt
1 tablespoon of sugar
1 tsp cinnamon
½ tsp nutmeg
8 slices stale challah bread, Brioche or other rich bread, sliced 1-inch thick
2 to 3 tablespoons butter, plus more for serving
Vegetable oil
Maple Syrup, fruit, nuts, whipped cream etc. for toppings

Beat eggs, half-and-half, salt, sugar, cinnamon, and nutmeg well with whisk. Pour mixture in a large shallow pan. Place bread slices in egg mixture and soak for 15-20 minutes, turning at the half way point.

Preheat electric griddle to medium heat. When bread has soaked up the egg mixture, lightly coat griddle with oil and butter. Cook pieces of toast 3-4 minutes on each side until lightly browned and edges are crisped. Top with your favorite maple syrup, fruit toppings, or powdered sugar.

Snickerdoodles

1 ½ cups white sugar
½ cup butter, softened
1 tsp vanilla
2 eggs
2 ¾ cups all-purpose flour
1 tsp cream of tartar
½ tsp baking soda
¼ tsp salt
½ tsp cinnamon

Preheat oven to 400 degrees F

Combine sugar, butter, vanilla, and eggs. Mix well.

Stir in flour, cream of tartar, baking soda, salt, and cinnamon. Blend well. Shape into 1 inch balls.

In a separate small bowl mix a 3 tablespoons sugar with 3 teaspoons cinnamon. Roll balls into mixture then place on an ungreased cookie sheet. Bake 8-10 minutes, until set. Immediately remove from cookie sheet to cooling rack.

Author Bio

Lilly York? How about Lilly Belle; a mis-plant northerner, living in a southern world. Southern charm is lost among late nights with a two year old granddaughter, heat flashes competing with hell, copious re-runs of *Murder She Wrote* with Jessica Fletcher catching the bad guy, and a vivid imagination keeping insanity at bay.

In both humor and mystery, Lilly draws inspiration from terrible twos, a 24 year old daughter who questions her sanity, a son who constantly spews bad puns, and a husband who has selective hearing. Though, that's perfectly alright with her, because what can you love more than a good laugh and a family so dysfunctional they almost seem functional?
Make sure you visit her at:

LillyYork.com

Made in the USA
Monee, IL
14 September 2020